John B. Renauld

Our Heroes

A military play - in five acts

John B. Renauld

Our Heroes
A military play - in five acts

ISBN/EAN: 9783337194321

Printed in Europe, USA, Canada, Australia, Japan

Cover: Foto ©Andreas Hilbeck / pixelio.de

More available books at **www.hansebooks.com**

A GRAND MILITARY ALLEGORY.

OUR HEROES.

A Military Play,

IN FIVE ACTS,

EIGHT ALLEGORICAL TABLEAUX AND TEN GRAND PICTURES,

INCLUDING

A THRILLING TRANSFORMATION TABLEAU.

TO WHICH ARE ADDED,

A DESCRIPTION OF THE COSTUMES—CAST OF THE CHARACTERS—EN-
TRANCES AND EXITS—RELATIVE POSITIONS OF THE PER-
FORMERS ON THE STAGE, AND THE WHOLE
OF THE STAGE BUSINESS.

By JOHN B. RENAULD,

Author of "Struck Blind," "Pablo," etc., etc.

TIME AND PLACE—THE SOUTHERN REBELLION.

NEW YORK:
ROBERT M. DE WITT, PUBLISHER,
No 33 ROSE STREET.

CHARACTERS.

UNION.

Wild Dan (Dan Sanford, a Scout, afterwards Captain U. S. V.)..

Harry Woodruff (Color Bearer, afterwards Colonel U. S. V.).

Mr. Woodruff (his Father, a Civilian).....................

Jack Woodruff (Harry's Brother, afterwards Captain)......

Benny Simmons (a Yankee, afterwards Sergt. Simmons)....

Capt. Grey (a Union Prisoner in Saulisbury)..............

Dr. Bolus (Stay-at-home Patriot and a "Cripple")..........

Mr. Stewart (the Village Banker)........................

Timothy O'Brien (a Milesian, true to his adopted country)..

Carl Schmidt (a native of the beautiful Rhine, and the Bunkmate of Timothy O'Brien)....................

Jeff (A 1 Cook)........ ....

Pompey (a colored Citizen)............ ....

Officer (commanding Troops at departure, etc., afterwards General)..

Orderly Sergeant.......................................

Father Tom (an old Refugee)............................

Clergyman...

Rev. Amasa Goodkind.................................

Alice Stewart (the Banker's Daughter)..................

Mehitable (Hired Help, Benny's Sweetheart).............

Mrs. Woodruff (Harry's Mother)........................

Mrs. Sanford (Dan's Wife)............................

Little Mary (Dan's Child).............................

REBEL.

Richmond Magruder (afterwards Captain C. S. A.).........

Rebel Scout (Bearer of the Dispatches)....................

Reuben Scrubbs (afterwards Corporal)....................

Dick.. ....

Rebel Officer..

Rebel Sergeant..

Rebel Guard (Saulisbury prison)........................

Hon. John Bragg......................................

Ladies, Children, Volunteer Troops, Citizens, Rebel Soldiers, Prisoners, etc.

SYNOPSIS OF INCIDENTS.

Act I.—BREAKING OUT OF THE WAR.

SCENE 1.—The Village Banker's Home. The Patriot's Council. Tim O'Brien's opinion of the Secessionists. Harry Woodruff Volunteers. Our Country Cousin's *debut* - "Yours, truly." Dr. Bolus, the stay-at-home patriot. Love and Labor. Richmond Magruder's Love. Alice Stewart's Loyalty. *Scene 11.*—Mehitable in Search of Benny. *Scene 111.*—Enlisted. Parental Sacrifice and Devotion to the Union. A Mother's Injunction: "Meet the foe; help carry our dear flag to victory. * * * Honor ever awaits the true soldier." *Scene IV.*—Africa on the War Path. Tripped Up. Benny "a-going for a Soldier." "Yours, truly." *Scene V.*—Presentation of the Flag to the Regiment. Alice Stewart's Caution to Harry as an old Schoolmate. True Love's Dawning. Benny and Mehitable. Magruder Receives his Answer, and Discloses his Treason. Alice Spurns the Traitor; the Latter's **Threats:** "I'll fight for the South, and ere long, a flag, wrought by hands as fair will be presented to me." Departure of the Regiment. MOTHER AND SON Tableau: **A MOTHER'S OFFERING TO LIBERTY.**

Between Scenes 5th and 6th, a lapse of one month occurs.

Scene VI.—Scrubb's Opinion of the Yankees. *Scene VII.*—Hon. John Bragg as a Fire-eater. Magruder in the South. Wild Dan's Answer. The Rebels Threaten to Hang Him. "Hold your Hosses." Dan's Unionism. "Oh, would that the Heavens might open and show you your country's flag!" Tableau: **THE GODDESS OF LIBERTY.** "The proud banner of Liberty! The flag that was never carried to defeat—don't raise your hands against its sacred folds. Beware! the North rises like one man!" **Transformation Tableau: THE RISING OF THE NORTH.** "Armies after armies will come down upon you! Legions of good men and true, who will fight like tigers, and never cease battling till the old flag is restored to its unsullied purity!"

Act II.—IN THE FIELD.

SCENE I.—**The Union Camp at Reveille.** Morning Roll Call. Ireland and Germany. Carl's Droobles. The Army Breakfast. Company Drill. Benny Simmons and his "raw recruits." *Scene II.*—THE UNION SCOUT DRIVEN FROM HOME. *Scene III.*—The Old Refugee's Flight. Burning of his Hut on the Mountain. Waylaid and Robbed. Wild Dan to the Rescue. DEATH IN THE MOONLIGHT. The Flag. *Grand Picture: THE SILENT OATH. Scene IV.*—Cripple and Lover. A Lover's Strategy Unavailing. *Scene V.*—Home of Alice. Meeting of the Lovers. Departure of Alice on her Mission of Charity: "If I can but succeed in making one poor soldier's last hour comfortable, I shall feel that I have done something to be proud of." *Scene VI.*—The Scouts. Pursued. Dan on the Trail. *Scene VII.*—"Hold your hosses." Struggle for the Dispatches. Wild Dan Overpowered. Rebel Justice: "I'm going to shoot you like a dog." "Ready!" "Aim!" Assistance at Hand. The Tables Turned. THE UNION SCOUT'S VICTORY. Tableau: **EMANCIPATION.**

Act III.—THE BATTLE.

SCENE I.—**Union Camp-Ground.** Tim and Carl Disagree. Benny Simulates. "Yours, truly." Carl's Droobles Again. Wild Dan as a Peace-maker. The Report of the Scout. "You may have saved the army from total defeat." *Scene II.*—**The Picket Line.** Carl Walking Post. "The putiful rain." Approach of Danger. Narrow Escape of Jeff. *Scene III.*—Magruder and his Blasted Hopes. Villainy's Plotting. Alice Heard of. Magruder's Dark Resolve. *Scene IV.*—**Grand Battle Scene.** Advance of the Union Troops. Meeting of the Armies. Desperate Struggle for the Colors. *Jack Woodruff's last Blow.* RESCUE OF THE COLORS BY HARRY WOODRUFF. GRAND CHARGE. Tableau: **VICTORY.**

Act IV.—THE BATTLEFIELD—SAULISBURY.

SCENE I.—**The Battlefield by Moonlight.** Magruder Among the Wounded. Tim O'Brien's Noble-heartedness. The Army Nurses. ABDUCTION OF ALICE. Attempted Rescue. Captured. "Yours, truly." "Yours, dru...... nary a dime." *Scene II.*—Wild Dan's Generous Resolve. *Scene III.*—From the Battlefield to Saulisbury Prison Pen. Dying of Hunger and Thirst. The Rebel's Proposal. "Take back your bread—death a thousand times rather than turn traitor to my country." Sharing a Crust of Bread. Jack Woodruff's Thoughts of Home. Tableau: **THE LOVED ONES AT HOME.** The Dead Line. The Fatal Shot. DEATH OF THE BRAVE. Tableau: **THE CROWNING OF THE AMERICAN SOLDIER.** *Scene IV.*—Jeff's War Experience. Benny Hears of the Capture of Alice. Plan for her Rescue. *Scene V.*—The Rebel Camp. The Dream of a Guilty Conscience. The Prisoner's Scorn for Proffered Love. Wild Dan on the Look-out. The Last Appeal. Insult to the old

Flag. A Brave Girl's Heroism. THE MOUNTAIN. Danger of Alice. THE PRECIPICE. Timely Arrival of Dan. *Grand Picture: RESCUE.*

Act V.—PATRIOTISM'S REWARD.

SCENE I.—Bummers on a Foraging Expedition. The Clergyman's Sermon. "Peruse, gentlemen, peruse." The Contrast. Outwitted Rebels. Benny's Idea and consequent Prisoners. *Scene II.*—The Army Homeward Bound. The German's Song. *Scene III.*—Jeff's Return. Col. Woodruff's Trunk. Pompey Entrapped. Dan after his Darlings. *Scene IV.*—HOME AGAIN. Alice and her Father. **The Soldier's Bride.** *Scene V.*—On Crutches. Jeff, Carl, and Tim O'Brien. The Latter's Conundrum. *Scene VI.*—The Church. Villainy's Dastardly Purpose. Return of the Regiment. Benny "pops" the Question. Alice and Harry. THE WEDDING. Attempted Murder. Wild Dan on Hand. Retribution. DEATH OF MAGRUDER. True Love's Reward. Dan and his Family. Peace and Happiness. **Grand and Impressive Tableau: OUR HEROES' TRIUMPH.**

SCENIC PLOT.

ACT I.—*Scene 1st.* Sitting-room in Mr. Stewart's residence, in fourth; sofa, chairs, etc.—richly furnished; door at back. Scene 2d.—Street in first. Scene 3d.—Interior of Farm House, in third, modestly furnished. Scene 4th.—Street in first. Scene 5th.—Landscape (or Village Square), in fifth (full stage).—Scene 6th.—Wood in first. Scene 7th.—Landscape in fifth (full stage), barrel near L. 4 E.

ACT II.—*Scene 1st.*—Camp scene—tents; camp-fire near R. U. E.; kettles of coffee over fire; arms stacked at doors of tents, etc.; (full stage). Scene 2d.—Landscape in third; exterior of hut, or Farm House, at R. 2 E. Scene 3d.—Moonlight landscape (full stage), set rocks, etc. Scene 4th.—Street in first. Scene 5th.—Parlor in third; door and windows at back; sofa, tables, chairs, etc.; train of cars seen in the distance—where train is not available, a train whistle should be heard when called for in the dialogue. Scene 6th.—Wood in first. Scene 7th.—Landscape (full stage), set rocks, etc.

ACT III.—*Scene 1st.* Camp scene, as Scene 1st., Act II. Scene 2d.—Opened landscape in third; rain. Scene 3d.—Wood in Second; rock at L. U. E. Scene 4th—Moonlight landscape. (same as Scene 3d., Act II). Moonlight not used.

ACT IV.—*Scene 1st.* Same as Scene 4th, Act 3d (with moonlight). Scene 2d.—Wood in first. Scene 3d.—Landscape at back; prison stockade across stage in third; sunlight. Scene 4th.—Wood in first. Scene 5th—Run to third from back of stage at L.; Precipice at R. of run, opposite L. 4 E.: tent flat at R. 2 E.; tent flats at L.

ACT V.—*Scene 1st.* Wood in second. Scene 2d.—Landscape in fourth; tent at R. 2 E.; camp-fire in centre. Scene 3d.—Street in first. Scene 4th.—Parlor in Mr. Stewart's residence, richly furnished, in third. Scene 5th.—Same as Scene 3d. Scene 6th.—Landscape (full stage); Exterior of church at L., with door at R. 3 E.; flag staff at L. U. E.

☞ Dark stage for all Tableaux.

COSTUMES.

WILD DAN (30 years). *Act I.*—Broad-brimmed slouch hat, and long, curly hair; long homespun, brown or gray, coat, or an Indian trapper's coat, with fringe, etc.; pants, inside of boot-legs, of same material as coat; neck bare; shirt of dark color, with wide collar, arranged over the coat collar, so as leave the front partially open, and expose the upper portion of the chest. *Act II*—Same as *Act I.* *Act III.*—Confederate dress. Gray cap, a long gray coat, belt and pistols—the coat should go down to boot-tops, so as to hide pants and blue blouse; when the gray coat is thrown off, it reveals the blue blouse and pants. *Act IV.*—

Scenes 2d and 4th.—Blue scout's dress, as revealed in the 3d Act. In first part of Scene 5th.—Confederate disguise; when he appears for the rescue disguise should be thrown off. Act V.—U. S. A. captain's uniform.

HARRY WOODRUFF (24 years). Act I.—Scene 1st.—Civilian's dress, such as a farmer's son would wear. Scene 3d.—U. S. A. fatigue uniform, with sergeant's stripes. Acts II. and III.—Lieutenant's uniform. Act IV.—Captain's uniform. Act V. —Colonel's uniform.

MR. WOODRUFF (60 years).—Farmer's best dress. Black or brown coat and pantaloons, Kossuth hat, high collar and wide black tie; white wig. For Act V., add white gloves.

JACK WOODRUFF (30 years). Act I.—U. S. A. fatigue uniform. Act III.—Captain's uniform. Act IV.—Tattered and torn pantaloons and shirt.

BENNY SIMMONS (25 years). Act I.—Scene 1st.—Farmer's field dress; a little eccentric, if desired. Scene 5th.—U. S. A. uniform. Act II.—U. S. A. sergeant's uniform, till end of play.

CAPT. GREY (30 years).—Similar dress to that of JACK WOODRUFF in prison scene.

DR. BOLUS (35 or 40 years).--Black felt hat, black coat and pantaloons.

MR. STEWART (50 years). Gray wig. Act I.—Neat business suit. Act II.—Same as Act I. Act V.—Fashionable black dress-coat and pants, white vest, white gloves.

TIM O'BRIEN (25 years). Act I.—Scene 1st.—Red wig. Short jacket, black or brown cap; pantaloons inside of boot-tops. Scene 5th.—Red wig, and eccentric U. S. A. uniform, till last scene of play, when he should re-appear in civilian's dress, with the exception of pants (which should be army pants), and on crutches.

CARL (25 years).—Misfitting U. S. A. uniform all through the play.

JEFF. Act I—Scene 4th.—Old silk hat, misfitting black coat and pants, large red tie, and blue vest; walking cane. Any amount of brass jewelry. Scene 5th, till last scene of the play.—Blue blouse and pants, and civilian's hat. In last scene of the play, same dress as in Act I., Scene 4th.

POMPEY.—Shabby farm-hand dress. Pantaloons in boot-tops; a whip.

OFFICER. Act I.—Colonel's Uniform. Act III.—General's uniform.

OLD REFUGEE (65 years).—Broad-brimmed slouch hat, gray preferable, long homespun coat and pants, of dark color. White wig.

REFUGEES.—Dress to correspond with that of OLD REFUGEE.

CLERGYMAN (45 years).—Long hair. Long coat and silk hat; no beard. The dress and hair of a dark color, would be more appropriate.

REV. AMASA GOODKIND.—Plain black dress.

PRISONERS, in Saulisbury.—Ragged dress.

ALICE STEWART (20 years). Act. I—Scene 2d.—Handsome and rich home dress.—Scene 5th.—Elegant walking dress. Act II.—Plain travelling suit. Act IV.—Army nurse dress. Act V.—Rich wedding dress.

MRS. WOODRUFF (60 years).—Plain black country home dress. White wig.

MRS. SANFORD (30 years). Act II.—Modest homespun dress. Act V.—Black alpaca dress; no silks if possible.

LITTLE MARY (10 years). Act II.—Homespun dress. Act V.—White dress.

MEHITABLE (20 years).—Plain country dress—odd in color and style, if desired.

GODDESS OF LIBERTY.—White dress; sash, cap, etc.

RICHMOND MAGRUDER (25 years). Act I.—Scenes 2d. and 5th.—Fashionable broadcloth suit, white vest, silk hat, dark colored gloves. Scene 7th.—Rebel captain's uniform. Act 5th.—Civilian disguise.

REUBEN SCRUBBS (25 years). Act I.—Scenes 6th and 7th —Rebel private's uniform --afterwards, add corporal's stripe.

HON. JOHN BRAGG (50 years).—Gray wig.—Homespun dress, coat and pantaloons—large black tie, and high collar, and gray slouch hat; large red handkerchief—spectacles.

REBEL OFFICER, SERGEANT, GUARD, and DICK.—In Confederate uniforms, to conform with their respective ranks.

PROPERTIES.

ACT I.—A Portmanteau ; two letters ; two knapsacks ; a dusting brush ; a whip ; a rich U. S. flag ; a barrel ; a Rebel flag ; thirty-two shields and spears.

ACT II.—Two camp kettles ; tin cups and plates ; a large bone ; a pack of cards ; stage money ; a blanket (army) ; tin basins ; pipes ; 6 U. S. fatigue blouses and caps ; a six-foot staff ; a bunting U. S. flag ; two band-boxes ; a small satchel ; a letter in envelope ; a roll of paper for dispatches ; a small rope, 6 ft. long ; shackles.

ACT III.—Two camp kettles ; stage money ; a tin basin ; a jack-knife ; roll of paper for dispatches ; a small whistle ; a torn U. S. flag, guns, caissons, etc.

ACT IV.—Broken caissons ; upturned guns ; muskets ; cartridge-boxes ; canteens, etc. ; a stretcher ; a pail ; crusts of black bread ; a loaf of fresh bread ; a bunting U. S. flag.

ACT V.—Fowls of all kinds, hams, vegetables, etc. ; a bottle labelled " Old Rye Whiskey " ; a plain black bottle ; canteens ; an old white hat ; a long linen duster ; a pack of cards ; a carpet bag ; a small trunk ; a pair of crutches ; a bowie knife.

NOTES.

IN Act I., when the dimensions of the stage, or any other cause, precludes the possibility of representing the Transformation Tableaux, the first part of it—" The Goddess of Liberty," may be omitted ; but " The Rising of the North " should begin where marked in the text.

In Act II., immediately preceding the company drill, a fancy or bayonet drill may be introduced.

In the Battle Scene, two pieces of artillery may be introduced just after the retreat of the Union skirmish line, taking care to have one piece captured by the Union troops, and leaving the other for the stage setting of Scene 1st, Act IV.

In Act IV., when scenery for the Precipice cannot be secured—substitute a wide bridge across back of stage, behind set rocks.

To give increased effect to the Battle Scene, imitation bomb-shells should be used.

The scene of " The Battlefield by moonlight," cannot be complete without wounded and dead soldiers personators.

TO THE PUBLIC.

IN a play designed to picture the most thrilling and patriotic events of our civil war, to be true to history, and, at the same time entertaining, when these same events have so often been recited to the reading public, is a difficult task. On the other hand, the perplexity is aggravated by the almost endless acts of heroism performed by the Union soldiers, in their efforts to check and conquer a rebellion as desperate in its struggle as it was wicked in its aim. The author must pause before the number of their sacrifices and deeds of bravery, as well as before the fiendish modes of persecution invented by the Confederates, which furnish the subject of the darkest page of their history. The limited space of a drama permits of the introduction of but few of them, but these should be selected with a right sense of the public taste. Patriotism, which so filled our volunteers' hearts ; bravery, which so characterized their warfare ; self-sacrifice, which was their constant virtue ; and suffering, which was their inevitable lot, as well as the heroism and self-abnegation of our women, which so often gladdened the hearts of the soldiers, and cheered them on to further deeds of valor—should find a place in a play founded on the events of the late war, however slight the reference may be. At the same time, the humorous side of the Union camp-life should be portrayed,—to omit that, would be to imply that it was all cheerless, while the fact is, that many a mirthful hour was spent around the camp-fire and soup-kettle.

In " Our Heroes " it has been endeavored to meet these requirements. Let the public judge. If it teaches a patriotic lesson, it will have accomplished its mission.

JOHN B. RENAULD,
GEORGE B. SQUIRES,
EDWIN A. PERRY,
Sole Proprietors.

EDWIN A. PERRY,
GEORGE B. SQUIRES,
Comrades, G. A. R., Managers.

Address : Managers " Our Heroes,"
Care of Irwin & Sons,
43 Wall Street, New York City.

SPECIAL NOTICE.

OUR HEROES.

ACT I.

SCENE I.—*Residence of* MR. STEWART, *the village banker; richly furnished. Door at back.*

MR. STEWART, MR. WOODRUFF, DR. BOLUS, *and numerous other* GUESTS, *discovered shaking hands. Some are seated.*

MR. STEWART. The news is bad, indeed; but what can we do? If a brother turns traitor and strikes the first blow, must we stand aside and give him full sway of the land wherein to perpetuate his rebellious designs?

MR. WOODRUFF. I say, no! Let every man of us join in the defence of our country.

DR. BOLUS. Now, friends, you're in too much of a hurry; don't get excited. These Southerners you talk about, were going to shoot Lincoln if we elected him, but they didn't do it. They fear us. (*egostically strutting, and displaying agility*) Don't be alarmed. And then, why do we interfere? The " Wide Awakes "—the young men—should do all the fighting.

MR. S. But we must take the initiative in this matter, and complete the organization of our regiment at once. If we must stay to care for our wives and daughters, we can, at least, give our money to help organize our sons to do battle for the old flag.

DR. B. My son is going. (*aside*) To sell hay for the army.

MR. W. But, say, Doctor, won't you go?

DR. B. I can't—what would become of my patients? Besides, I am a cripple, (*limps*) and——

MR. W. Rather suddenly, Doctor. Eh?

DR. B. Oh, no! I've been a cripple since I was a baby; but it only comes on violently when the weather is bad.

MR. W. And when the country is in danger.

DR. B. Mr. Woodruff, your remarks are not pleasant.

MR. S. Come, friends, we must not quarrel here. There will be plenty of that to do down South.

MR. W. All right, Mr. Stewart; but what I say here, I'll back up down there, if need be. As long as me and my boys live, Old Abe won't go a-begging for volunteers.

Enter HARRY *and* TIM, *at back.*

MR. S. (*to* HARRY *and* TIM). Good morning, gentlemen; you are most welcome. We were talking about volunteers for our regiment which departs in a few days.

HARRY. A noble move in the right direction, Mr. Stewart. (MR. WOODRUFF *rubs his hands with glee.*)

MR. S. And will you join ?

HAR. Certainly I will.

MR. W. I told you he would. (*rubs his hands with increased force.*)

HAR. No young man should refuse to offer his life for the protection of our dear country. Only a coward or a traitor would do so. We should stand firm through the storm and remain true to the constitution of our forefathers. Honor to the man who inherits such patriotism, for it is with such men that we can uphold the honor and integrity of our country, redeemed from thraldom by him whose name is immortal—Washington!

MR. W. (*grasps* HARRY's *hand*). Well said, my brave boy—well said! Those words make me happy. God will bless you for them. Your brother Jack writes that he is coming to join the regiment too.

TIM O'BRIEN. Yes, Mr. Shtewart, and if yez want me, ye can have me. Faith, put me name down this blessed minit. Ameriky is only me adopted country, but I'll fight for her—yes, give her the last dhrop of me blood.

MR. S. You're a brave boy, Tim.

TIM. Shure, and it isn't in the O'Briens to be cowards—they're always ready to lick a durty blackguard, and thim rebels are blackguards, to try to brake up this country. Ough! Gorry! bad luck to thim any way! (*retires up.*)

DR. B. (*aside*). It don't hurt an Irishman to get killed.

Enter BENNY SIMMONS, *at back; carries a bag. Takes a chair from* DR. BOLUS, *who is about to sit on it, and sits down;* DR. BOLUS *on the floor, is assisted up by some of the* GUESTS. BENNY *places bag and hat near chair.*

MR. S. Why, Benny! Good morning!

BENNY. Yours truly, uncle.

MR. S. What brings you here so unexpectedly ?

DR. B. (*angrily*). Why did you—why——

BEN. Take a rest, old mortar and pestle manipulator. (*to* MR. STEWART) You want to know what brought me here ? Shank's mare and the war, by the 'tarnal !

MR. S. (*grasping his hand*). Nephew, do you mean to say that you've come here to join the boys who are going to fight the rebels ?

BEN. I mean to say that I'm a-going to take a hand in cooking the goose of this 'ere secesh business.

MR. S. Nephew, you are a brave fellow; and I can assure you, that when old men are wanted, I will go willingly.

BEN. (*rising and shaking his uncle's hand*). Uncle, you're a brick !

MR. S. (*naively and doubtingly*). No ?

BEN. You're tougher 'n cheap beefsteak. Uncle, look me in the eye; do I look skeered ?

MR. S. Not in the least.

BEN. You bet. Then I'll 'list, and fight them 'tarnal rebels. Put my name down for a——

MR. S. A captain ?

BEN. No, sir; nary a time. Put me down for a private. I can fight for and win a captaincy, but ain't a-going to beg it.

MR. S. Well, come, we must prepare for the departure of the regiment, when the colors are to be presented.

Dr. B. I have a few patients to visit; so you will excuse me to our friends, if I am not present.

Mr. W. (*aside*). Anything to get out of it.

Har. Let us see that every able-bodied man responds to your call, gentlemen.

Ben. (*to* Harry, *grasping his hand*). Yours, truly.

Mr. S. Come, friends, let us proceed to the Town Hall to complete our work of organization.

Omnes. Yes, yes.

[*All exit at back—*Tim *and* Benny *last—meeting in door.*

Enter Mehitable, *at* R., *with a duster in one hand, and a letter in the other.*

Mehitable (*going about dusting*). Wall, now, we're going to have war, and a big one, too. Them rebels are bound to break up this country. Are they, though? Wall, I guess they won't. I'll go down there myself, and thrash 'em to a jelly, before they'll do it, the nasty things! Let me see what my Benny has got to say about it. By the by, he ought to be here to-day. I ain't seen him for a whole week. (*reads letter*) " Mehit." (*speaks*) That's me. (*reads*) " As they say in yaller-kivered books, ' Love, I'm coming.' " (*speaks*) Benny must have been drinking, to write such nonsense. (*reads*) " And I'm going down South to whip them 'tarnal rebels." (*speaks*) I guess he kin jest do it. He ain't skeered of anything. I don't like the idea of losing my Benny; but, then, he may be a Kernel —oh! me. Jest think of it—Mrs. Kernel Benjamin Franklin Simmons. Wouldn't I put on airs, though? (*looking off at* R.) Here comes Miss Alice and her beau—the sick loviers. If there's anything in the world I despise it's a lovier that's always sighing like this, (*sighs*) or puts on a face like this, as though he was going to cry. Here they come—two is company, but three is a crowd—that's what Benny says when we're in the garden alone. I guess he's right—so I might as well vamose.

[*Exit,* L.

Enter Alice, *holding letter in her hand, and* Richmond, R. 2 E.

Richmond. Well, you do not mean to keep me in suspense until the war is over? It may last for years.

Alice. Then I may keep you waiting for years.

Rich. You are cruel. May I hope that your decision will be altered before that time?

Alice. I cannot tell the future; but my intention is to devote my days to the cause of my country. If I cannot carry a musket, I can, at least, do my best to cheer on the brave boys who go forth to stake their lives as the price of a re-united country.

Rich. I admire your patriotism. (*aside*) I hate it.

Alice. Will you not join the army?

Rich. It is my intention to do so. Yet, Miss Stewart, listen to me, do not refuse me—at least, give me hope. My love for you is soul-deep; your image fills my thoughts when I awake; in my sleep, it is the angel of my dreams.

Alice. You forget that I owe my utmost obedience to my father.

Rich. He will not oppose your choice, I know.

Alice. Besides, time is a wonder-worker, and with it the deepest love sometimes changes into indifference.

Rich. With me it could not be so. I would be your slave.

Alice. But give me time to reflect—a woman may not know her own heart at a moment's notice.

Rich. Then I may hope?

Alice. It is a faint heart that despairs, yet I would not say hope.

Rich. (*aside*). All hope is not lost. (*aloud*) Will you permit me to escort you to the departure of the regiment?

Alice (*hesitating*). Y—yes, sir.

Rich. Then good morning.

Alice. Good morning, sir. (*retires to right, reading letter she held in her hand on entering.*)

Rich. (*aside*). I'll try devotion, still.   [*Exit at back.*

SCENE II.—*A Street.*

Mehitable (*outside*). I'll be back in a minit. I'm only going to the Town Hall.

Enter, L., hurriedly, putting on shawl and bonnet.

That Benny has been to the house—I know he has, for I found his portmantoo outside the door of the sitting-room; and he didn't see me—he went down to the Town Hall. I'm going down there, too, and I'll give him a piece of my mind—he's jest like all the rest of the men, full of promises, but never comes up to time. Didn't he swear he'd lose his star that lost its glim—glimmer, or something like that—anyway, it was something fearful he'd lose before he'd forget me; and now he comes here and don't even try to see me, but runs off with the rest to join the regiment. Now, suppose I'd make love to sum of them saucy fellows in the village, would he like it? Wall, I guess not—I guess he'd get up sum kind of a funeral; but I'm after him—I won't get up a funeral, but I'll make him think there's a powerful dance a-going on about him.

                    [*Exit, R.*

SCENE III.

Home of Mr. Woodruff, *modestly furnished.*   Mrs. Woodruff *in a chair,* Mr. Woodruff *near her;* Jack *speaking to her, and* Harry *packing his knapsack at back, discovered.*

Mrs. Woodruff (*to* Jack). Ah! my son, little do you know of the sorrows that fill a mother's heart at such a parting as this.

Mr. W. Come, cheer up, old 'ooman! The boys are only going to do their duty.

Jack. Yes, mother; and we won't be away long. Every able-bodied man in this town should turn out to fight the rebels. My dear wife bade me God speed, although it was hard for her to give me up, while the little darlings clung to me in tears.

Mrs. W. God will guard and bless your darlings. You are right, those bad men should be punished.

Jack. Punished! Every one of them should be——

Mrs. W. (*stops him*). Do your duty, Jack, and God will not abandon you.

Jack. I will, mother; your good counsels shall not be forgotten, and I'll never abandon my country as long as she needs me. (*retires up, to pack his knapsack.*)

Har. (*comes down*). Here I am. My knapsack's ready, and I must go, or the regiment will leave without me.

Mrs. W. Then you, too, must leave me! (*weeps*)

Har. Come, dear mother; dry your eyes. You would not wish me to stay—to forsake my country, in this, the hour of her great peril?

Mrs. W. Ask you to stay? No, Harry; I say, go! meet the foe—

help carry our dear flag to victory! It is hard for me to part with you
—I fear my heart will break; but no, it will not—a mother's heart
must live for the children who volunteer in the defence of their country's
honor.

HAR. Noble words, mother dear; and I shall ever cherish them in
my heart. (MR. WOODRUFF *and* JACK *come down*) Oh, mother! I shall
never find love like yours—never find so true a friend. And you, father, how dearly I'll remember you.

JACK. And so will I, father.

MR. W. Take my blessing, my boys—I—I——— *hides his tears.*)

MRS. W. Come closer, my children, and listen to me. I shall not be
near you to console and comfort you, but I will send many a prayer to
God for the safety of the absent ones. Remember your duty to your
country; above all, never flinch in its performance. Honor ever awaits
the true soldier. Take my blessing. (HARRY *and* JACK *kneel*) May Heav-
en watch over you and return you in safety to a mother's heart; may
He who traces our destinies, hasten the day when we can once more
greet the flag of freedom, unfurling its broad stripes to the breeze, waft-
ing the glad tidings of peace over our dear country, which owes its
honor, its grandeur (*rising*) to Him alone! (*blesses her children as she looks
up. Scene closes on Tableau*)

SCENE IV.—*A Street.*

Enter JEFF, L.

JEFF. Golly, dis am a mighty thing—dis goin' to de war. Fightin'
runs in my family. My gran'-fadder fell fightin' in the reb'lutionary
struggle. I fell fightin' once—when I had de row with dat odder nigger. Golly, how that nigger did butt! Ough!

Enter POMPEY, R.

Halloa, nigger, whar am you goin' to.

POMPEY. Goin'! Goin' to fight.

JEFF. Ain't goin' to de war, is you? Eh?

Enter BENNY, R., *who listens.*

POMP. Yes, I is.

JEFF. Did de doctor examabine you; am you all right about de
chawers; eh?

POMP. Yes. But say, Jeff, what am de pill man gwine to do wid you?

JEFF Gwine to do wid me? He's dun gone dun it already. This 'ere
pusson's gwine to be de—de—malufactrer of hard tack chowder for de
troops; den I'se gwine to be promulgated to an ossifer. Golly, nigger,
you's no whar.

POMP. You fight? Ough! You fight? Hush, nigger, you wouldn't
fight a flea!

JEFF. I'se gwine to fight de rebels, and when I get down dar, I'll
shoot de fust man I meets, right fru de gizzard, and I'll be so brave that
my name 'll be passed down to de generations of prosperity. Eh? Golly! in de words of———

BENNY (*tripping them up*). Yours truly.

JEFF. Don t! Golly, Massa Benny, you's powerful strong in de foot!

BEN. Didn't mean to hurt you, Jeff; but the pesky doin's of them ar
'tarnal rebels have jest set my blood b'ilin' like all possessed, and I jest
feel like mashing somebody.

JEFF. Well, please don't let the exuberiance of your—your—you know?

BEN. Oh, yes. I guess that's all right.

POMP. You might let a fellah know when you mean to knock him down.

BEN. I will, the next time—but to-day I feel like all possessed. It's darn mean to leave Mehit jest as I was about to pop the question.

JEFF. Mr. Simmons, Mehit's your gal? You's awful on gals.

BEN. You're jest right, Jeff. Gals is sweeter than punkin pie.

JEFF. Does you know, Mr. Simmons, dis ere cullud pusson was allus powerful on gals? Wunst I made love to another fellah's gal Ough! as they say in the song—afore I could kiss her lily-white hand, that ar nigger jest went for my wool.

BEN. Now, hold on, Jeff; you're a-gettin' eloquent. You're a sweet-looking nigger to make love to a lily-white hand. (*knocks his hat over his eyes*) I guess 'most any gal would rather have the measles and the small-pox than have you. (*going L*) Good-bye, Jeff—good-bye, Pompey.

[Exit, L., singing.

POMP. Say, nigger, how's yer head?

JEFF. How's yer back? Golly, what a gentle lubber he is. Pompey, dem fellahs all tink dere gals in lub wid dis 'ere cullud pusson. Dat cums from being good-looking.

POMP. Shut up, and come along.

JEFF. All right, snoozer.   *[Both exit at R., singing.*

I'se gwine to jine de band—
Oh! de jub'lee am cum;
I'll take my sw—ord in hand—
But I'll neber leave hum.

SCENE V.—*Landscape.*

Enter troops, L. U. E.   Stage march.

FIRST MOVEMENT.

Marching in two ranks, at right shoulder shift arms (all movements to be made without doubling), by the flank, right in front. Enter L. U. E.; when left of company is uncovered, Col. commands, Break to the left in column of companies! Capt. of Co. commands 1st Co. by the left flank, march! (the steps should be very short—a little more than "mark time"). 2d and 3d Co.'s come on, executing same movement—head of column must preserve distance for company wheel. Col. commands, Head of column to the left! Capt. of Co. commands, 1st Co left wheel, march! when a full half wheel is made, Col. commands, 1st Co. by the right flank, by file left. Capt. of Co. repeats the order, 1st Co by the right flank, by file left, march! Exit, L. 1 E., reappearing, L. U. E, as at first. The instant the command march is given by Capt. of 1st Co., the Capt. of 2d Co commands, 2d Co, left wheel, march! balance of movement of 2d and 3d Co.'s same as 1st Co. (The wheeling should be executed slowly, so that right of Co. wheeling shall not strike left of Co. passing off by the flank.)

SECOND MOVEMENT.

When head of column has reached opposite side of stage (i. e, from L.

U. E. *to* R. U. E.), *Col. commands, Break to the left in column of platoons! Capt. of Co. commands,* 1st *platoon, by the left flank, march! Step should be slow and careful. Guide left! (without guide crossing over). Commanders of* 2d *platoons should be in rear of* 1st *platoons; when the break is made to the left they can wait for their platoon to come up, and execute same movement as* 1st *platoon. All orders by platoon com'ders should be loud and clear, not forgetting the "guide left." When the column of six platoons is complete, Col. commands, Head of column to the left! Comdr. of* 1st *platoon commands,* 1st *platoon, left wheel, march! when half wheel is made, Forward, march! almost in the same breath Col. commands again, Head of column to the left!* 1st *platoon executes another half wheel as before, which places them marching to rear of stage in column of platoons while rest are marching to front, repeating in succession orders and movements of* 1st *platoon. When the entire movement is completed, Col. commands, By platoons, by the right flank, by file left, march! (to head of line). File left, march!*

THIRD MOVEMENT.

When head of column has reached position, as in the two previous movements, Col. commands, Break to the left in column of companies! Capt. of 1st *Co. commands,* 1st *Co., By the left flank, march!* 2d *and* 3d *companies execute same movements as* 1st *Co. Care should be taken to preserve equal distance for companies—* 1st *company just in front of* 1st E., 2d *Co. at* 3d E., 3d *Co. at* U. E. *Col. commands, By company, by the right flank, countermarch by file left, march! When completed, Countermarch by file left, march! When completed—By company, by file left, march! To head of line, File left, march! When near* L. 1 E., *File left, march! Same at* L. U. E. *and* R. U. E. 1st *Co. on right of stage.* 2d *at back.* 3d *at left. Col. commands. Battalion, Halt! Front! Right Dress! Front! Order Arms! Parade rest!*

Enter young ladies, with flag carried by ALICE, *who is accompanied by* RICHMOND, R. U. E. *They take their position at left of* COLONEL, *who is in centre, opposite and facing color sergeant—when* ALICE *commences to speak,* COLONEL *faces her.*

ALICE (*holding flag in her hand*). 'Friends, allow me to present you with this flag in the name of the ladies of this town. It has been wrought by their hands, and moistened with their tears. We cannot follow you—we cannot share with you the hardships of the march, or the dangers of the conflict—but our prayers go with you for your safe return; and, with a deep sense of your heroism, we hopefully look to the future when through your bravery and self-sacrifice, this flag shall have been carried unsullied to victory, and brought back to your homes covered with glory—the harbinger of the blessings of a fruitful peace.

OFFICER (*commands*). Attention, Battalion! Shoulder arms! Color sergeant! to the front. March! Halt! (MISS STEWART *hands flag to* HARRY) Battalion, Present Arms! (*drums ruffle*) Battalion, shoulder arms! Order arms! Parade rest! (*villagers gather around the flag, and sing "Flag of the Free"*) On you, sergeant, devolves the duty of carrying this flag; and may the Regiment prove itself worthy of its ensign.

HARRY (*to* OFFICER). Permit me to say a few words?

OFFICER. Certainly.

HAR. Miss Stewart, and also the ladies of our beautiful town:—When away from you, during the great struggle we are about to enter upon, with the sound of contention in our ears, and the shout of liberty, mingled with prayers to God, on our lips, we, as American soldiers, will still remember that, at home, around the Northern firesides, are wives, daughters and sisters, whose love of country is deeply rooted in their heart's affections, and who stand before the world as examples of honor, patriotism, and virtue—the dearest treasures of a nation's love; and the thought will inspire us with new-born zeal in the performance of our duties as defenders of the dear old flag.

OFFICER. Many heartfelt thanks, ladies, for your kind wishes, and this beautiful gift. We did not seek strife, but there is a point where insult passes the bounds of endurance, and the Southern people, who have so long nursed their hatred for us, will soon be bowed down in sorrow by the strong arm of an indignant people, turned against them by their own false ambition. Never will we rest till this foul rebellion is laid low in the dust! Let our foes do their worst—they have sowed the wind, let them reap the whirlwind. Insult upon insult have they heaped upon us; day after day provocations have followed each other without interruption, until forbearance ceases to be a virtue; the day has come when we go, with sword in hand, to teach them lessons of loyalty to the proud banner they have insulted; the banner before which haughty England's red cross went down in defeat; the banner to which the world, gazing at us with admiration, paid the tribute of greatness; the flag around which has banded, for nearly a century, the mightiest, the freest people on earth; but with that same flag to guide and cheer us on, we will battle and conquer—adding one more wreath to the crown of glory which is the heritage of the true American soldier! (*commands*) Attention, Battalion. Color sergeant, about face! to your post. March! Battalion, shoulder arms! Right face! Arms port! Break ranks! March!

MR. W. (*to* HARRY). Well, my boy, we must soon part. May God bless you and bring you back in safety!

HAR. I trust we shall not be long separated; I hope to return soon. Come what may, we shall restore our dear land to peace, or find a soldier's grave. (MR. WOODRUFF *goes up stage.*)

RICH. (*approaches* ALICE). Miss Stewart——

ALICE. In a moment, sir.

HAR. (*to* ALICE). I value highly the fortune which makes me the bearer of this flag received at your hands. Since we were schoolmates I have hoped for an opportunity to prove to you how much I appreciate your good opinion, and now, going to battle for my native land, I will endeavor to so bear myself as to earn your esteem, which has so long been the aim of my life.

ALICE. Guard it with caution; for, while I shall glory in learning that it is carried to victory, I should deplore misfortune to its gallant bearer.

HAR. (*embarrassed*). But, see, Mr. Magruder wishes to speak to you.

ALICE. I would rather speak with you.

HAR. Then, may I hope?

ALICE. Yes.

RICH. (*approaching* ALICE). Miss Stewart; may I—— (ALICE *walks off with* HARRY *Aside*) She slights me. So, so!

BEN. Now, Mehit, don't forget to write every day.

MEHIT. No, Benny, I won't forget. You know I couldn't forget you.

BEN. (*seizing her hand*). Yours truly. (*they retire up*)

RICH. (*goes to* ALICE). Miss Stewart, I wish to speak to you.

ALICE. What do you wish to say, sir ?

RICH. You avoid me for——

ALICE. Excuse me, sir; but why are you not in the ranks with those brave men ?

RICH. My answer?

ALICE. I have no answer to give. You should join the regiment and serve your country.

RICH. (*with passion*). Then you have deceived me! But you shall pay dearly for it! Since you demand that I shall become a soldier, I answer you—I will! But not under that hated flag! I'll fight for the South, and ere long a scene, similar to this, will be enacted in a Southern clime—where a flag, destined to be the rallying standard of this country, and wrought by hands as fair, will be presented to me.

ALICE. Traitor! leave me. Your conduct leaves no doubt in my mind as to your *honor!* (*raising her voice, and* VILLAGERS, *etc., gathering round her*) I despise a traitor! The man who would thus side with rebels for love of gain, or self-aggrandizement, cannot be brave. Shame on you; to turn, like the viper, and sting the hand that warmed you into life. (SOLDIERS *manifest great discontent. Assembly sounds.*)

RICH. (*in rage, aside*). Foiled! But I'll be revenged. Curses on you all!   [*Exit,* L.

HAR. The bugle sounds. Good-bye, Alice; I thank you for the encouragement you have given me. Good-bye!

ALICE. Good-bye, Harry. (SOLDIERS *shake hands with* VILLAGERS. *Battalion forms.*)

OFFICER (*commands*). Attention, battalion! Shoulder arms! Present arms! Shoulder arms! Battalion, right face! Right shoulder shift! Forward, march! (TROOPS *file off stage. Music.*)

HAR. } (*as they pass their father and mother, fall out of the ranks, and*
JACK } *kiss them both*). Good bye!

MRS. W. Good bye, my sons, and may Heaven bless our cause! (HARRY *gives a last look to* ALICE, *and rejoins ranks with* JACK TIM *and* JEFF, *at the end.*)

TABLEAU.—"*A mother's offering to Liberty!*" *Between this scene and the following one, a lapse of one month is supposed to occur.*

SCENE VI.—*A Street.*

Enter REUBEN SCRUBBS *and* DICK, *with muskets,* L.

REUBEN SCRUBBS. Come along, Dick; the show 'll be over if we don't hurry up.

DICK. Say, Reub, what do you think of the war as a fuss—I think it's going to be all powerful hot.

SCRUBBS Nonsense, it's going to be over in a short time. We'll have more fun than at a quilting party, or at a sugar boiling.

DICK. I guess you're right, Reub. The Yankees can't fight like we uns. Eh ?

SCRUBBS. No, besides they haven't got enough men to send down here to whip us.

DICK. That's what old John Bragg says, and I reckon he ought to know.

SCRUBBS. There ain't a more knowing man in all Missouri. (*confidentially*) Why, he told me the other day that the whole Northern and Western States are coming down to us.

Dick. Coming down to us? How? To fight us, or help us?

Scrubbs. To help us, you cussed fool—and if they don't, a Southern man is worth two Yankees any day—that's what old John Bragg says, and I reckon he ought to know.

Dick. The Yankees haven't got any guns, have they?

Scrubbs. Nothing but old flint locks.

Dick. Have they got any war vessels? Any money?

Scrubbs. No, neither war vessels nor money. Floyd and Jeff Davis took care of the money and the ships before they got through with them fellows in Washington.

Dick. The Yankees don't know how to fight, do they? they never done any gun fighting?

Scrubbs. No. It was the South who done the fighting in the Revolution, and licked the English and the Mexicans not long ago.

Dick. Yes, and I'll bet we can do it again, with the Yankees added to them. Come, come, the show must be going on. (*both exit, R.*)

SCENE VII.—*Wood in Missouri.*

Rebel Soldiers *on right of stage facing left; one company, with* Scrubbs *and* Dick *on the right, at place rest with* Magruder *in front of centre.* Wild Dan *at L. 1 E.,* Citizens *on left of stage, huddled near 2d and 3d L. E. Rebel flag held by one of the ladies. Stump speaker on a barrel, opposite L. 3 E., just in front of crowd, addressing the soldiers, discovered.*

Hon. Jno. Bragg (*on barrel*). Friends! Brothers in a sacred cause! the hour has come! we have met to avenge the insults offered by a cowardly foe to our State! To protect our homes and our firesides! To raise a wall of fire, if need be, around our wives and daughters! To save them from the polluting touch of the ruthless invader! To rally round our flag, "the Stars and Bars"—the emblem of Liberty, and of the South! Is it necessary for me to recount to you all the causes that have driven our glorious country to this step? No! I know it is not; —the intelligence of the South knows that no other course is left us but to fight—if we are to deserve the name of men! And men we are— brave! true! free men! Men of the South! Men who will meet the Yankee mudsills of the North, "with bloody hands, and welcome them to hospitable graves." Our country is, indeed, a blooming garden—but it shall be made a graveyard for Northern hirelings, ere we desert the flag for which we have drawn our swords! (*takes flag and presents it to* Richmond) I present this flag to this brave man who left the North to fight for his native State; and may he guard it well!

Rich. Yes, friends! I did leave the North, where I was engaged in business; for, when the time came for me to choose between the South and the North—between Liberty and Oppression—between this flag and the hated symbol of Northern fanaticism—I left every thing to come among you, and draw my sword in defence of my native State. A few days before I left the North, I was present at a flag presentation—and because I dared to speak my sentiments, and declare my sympathy for the South, I was hooted at and spurned; but the cowards went no farther. I told them, then, that I should raise a regiment in the South—to which would be presented a flag wrought by fairer hands, destined to be the emblem of Liberty throughout the world! And I have kept my word! Under this flag we will battle for the South, until we bring the cursed Yankees to our feet—pleading for mercy! But we'll grant no mercy! What say you, men?

SOLDIERS. No! No!

RICH. Now, boys! Give a good cheer for Jeff Davis and the Southern Confederacy. (*all yell. To* DAN) What say you ? Will you join us ?

DAN. No, I won't !

SOLDIERS (*starting, as if to leave the ranks*). Hang him !—string him up.

DAN. Hold your hosses! (*to* RICHMOND) I heered you say, just now, that no violence was offered you. Now don't go to hanging me, before I've opened my mouth.

RICH. Go ahead, then ; but be brief.

DAN. You want to fight the Yankees?—what for ? what have they done to you ? The Yanks never done you any harm. In your mountains or in your cities, they never troubled you. If the Southern people wanted bread, the Yankees, like brothers, would be the first to offer it to them.

SOLDIERS. We don't want their bread.

DAN (*not noticing interruption*). You're going to lick 'em, are you ? Now, let me tell you it's going to be the toughest job you've undertaken in a long time. Don't you fight 'em—there's too many of 'em to make it comfortable—just lay down your arms and be brothers again. Go back to your homes and families and be contented under the dear old flag our fathers fought for ; and if any stranger dares to lift a finger against you, the Yanks will be the first to take your part But don't you fight 'em —don't you force 'em to fight you; for if you do, they'll come down on you like a hurricane, and sweep you off the face of the earth—carnage and blood will follow in their tracks—and where, now, all is peace, there will be nothing but desolation and ruin. This country ain't going to be divided, nohow—for God has made it the grandest country on the face of the earth! Oh! would that the heavens might open (*scene opens— Tableau : " The Goddess of Liberty" with the U. S. flag*) and show you your country's flag—the proud banner of Liberty ! the flag that was never carried to defeat! Don't raise your hands against its sacred folds ! Beware ! The North rises like one man—(*Transformation Tableau, showing children around the Goddess*) Armies after armies will come down upon you ! Legions of good men and true, (*Transformation Tableau, showing soldiers—and completing the picture*) who will fight like tigers, and never cease battling till the old flag is restored to its unsullied purity !

Grand Tableau—Curtain.

ACT II.

SCENE I.—*Landscape Tents. Fire near 5th* E. F., *kettle over it. Reveille sounds. Enter* ORDERLY SERGEANT, R. U. E., *who goes from tent to tent calling.* JEFF *nodding over fire.*

When the company forms for roll call it should do so from R 3 E. *to* L. 3 E. —*the same position should be observed by the company preparatory to starting for drill – the awkward squad on left of Co. Line for breakfast, should form with right resting near fire.*

ORDERLY. Turn out to Roll Call.

TIM, CARL *and* SOLDIERS *enter from tents right and left, and f rm line.*

Right dress, front, attention to roll call. (*calls roll, bringing in the names of* SERGEANT SIMMONS, TIM O'BRIEN *and* CARL. *Commands*) Right face ! Break ranks !   March !   [*Exit*, R. U. E.

Some SOLDIERS *converse ; some sit on the ground to amuse themselves ; others light their pipes and smoke. One or two exit and return with basins of water, and wash their hands and faces. Enter* LIEUT. HARRY WOOD-RUFF, L. U. E., *and comes down* C. *with* BENNY.

BENNY (*grasps* HARRY'S *hand*). Yours, truly.

HARRY. I start, to-day, for home, on a two weeks' furlough, and I want to say good-bye to you. Have you got any message to Mehitable ?

BEN. What in thunder are you going home for ?

HAR. Alice is bent on coming down this way as a nurse, and I'm to be her escort.

BEN. Oh ! you cuss, you ! How long has this thing been a-goin' on ?

HAR. What thing ? What do you mean ?

BEN. Why, a-making love to Alice Stewart.

HAR. Benny, you're crazy—I ain't making love to Alice. We were schoolmates, you know—and——

BEN. Schoolmates be darned ! Schoolmates ? Yours, truly ! Well, you would make a pretty pair of mates, that's so. All right, Harry. I'll go and write a letter to Mehit, and say that I've told you to kiss her for me ; but mind, don't you put in one for yourself—you and she wan't schoolmates, you know.

Exit HARRY, L. U. E., *and* BENNY, *into tent.* CARL *and* TIM *in centre, playing cards.*

CARL. You shust blay fair, und don't scheat.

TIM. All right. It's wid the likes of ye I like to play forty-five. A Dutchman play forty-five ! Gorra, bad luck to the Dutch !

CARL. Vat you say mit de Dietch ?

TIM. Go on. Play your cards, and never mind the Dutch.

CARL. Oh ! you be blaying foolishness mit me.

TIM. Arrah ! git out. Is it the likes of yes talks about fooling ? Ah ! git out wid ye ! since I left the ould dart, I never met such a crayther as yerself.

CARL. Is dot so ?

TIM. Yes ! now mind your cards, and ye won't say I chated ye. I'll bet ye sivinty-five cints I bate ye this game.

CARL. Vat's the matter mit you ?

TIM. I can bate ye.

CARL. Vat's dat ? You blay fair of the cards mit me, und I vins.

TIM. Sivinty-five cints ye don't.

CARL. Dot's all right. (*aside*) Dot Irishmans vas a humpug.

TIM. Down wid the stamps, Dutchy. (*they lay down money.*)

CARL. Of mine own gountry I vas a vine blayer.

TIM. The divil you say ? Look out ! I've got the ace.

CARL. Dish vos von Irish games ?

TIM. Yes, and I can bate you at it: look out—I've got the ace and the five fingers

CARL. I got swei ace. But, mein Gott, vat is dat five fingers. Eh ? (*examines his fingers.*)

TIM. Here it is—now play on.

CARL. (*eyeing him*). Dot five spots vas blayed of this game pefore.

TIM (*grabs the money*). The money is mine—and the divil a bit of chating did I do ayther.

CARL. Give dot monish by mineself. You vas a swindlemans. (*seizes* TIM. *who wrestles with him.* SOLDIERS *gather around, urging them on. Breakfast call sounds, and they separate. All rush for their cups and plates.*)

TIM. It's robbin' me this Dutchman would be after doin'. (*to* CARL) Arrah! by me sowl, I'll batter yer skull if yer not more gintlemanly wid me.

CARL (*brushing his hair with his sleeve*). Of mine gountry you vas a ropper, und you shust get hung dwo dimes. (*walks backward, upsets kettle over fire. and rolls about.*)

SOLDIERS. What are you doing? Get out! (*they toss h'm.*)

BEN. (*entering from tent*). Stop that nonsense, and fall in for coffee and meat.

TIM. Do ye hear that, Dutchy? Why don't ye lape for yer rights?

CARL. You vas make me doo much droubles by mine ownself, (*going up to* TIM *in a passion*) and you shust took a rest of by yourself. (*down c.*) Dot man vas a humpug. Irishmans vas all humpugs all der dimes. He vas make droubles by me alvays. Dis vorld vas peen full of droubles. Vonce upon a dime—und dot dimes vas not long avay—I hafe a frau. She vas pully gal—but dunder, she vas make droubles by my hair all der dimes——

BEN. Stop your noise, and fall in the ranks.

CARL. All raight, shargeant.

BEN. There's all the coffee that's left; now, go easy. (*the men crowd around and fill up their cups*) What in thunder do ye want to jam up that way for, ye darned hogs! Here's yer meat. (*deals out meat giving* TIM *a very large bone without any meat on it.* TIM *gets his rations first, then moves to the other end of the line, and tries to get another.* SOLDIERS *exit into tents as they are served*) See 'ere, Tim, you jest g't out. You can't play that game on me!

TIM. Faith, I thought ye was through wid de bones, and was giving out the mate. And is this all I'm going to have?

BEN. Is that all? Why, you greedy cuss, you can eat more than any six men in the company.

TIM. Oh! be the Moses! I thought ye gave me this for a wapon! And am I to ate this? Faith, an' it would take an alligator to make the print of his tathe in this. (*goes back grumbling, as the drill call sounds.*)

ORDERLY *enters*, R. U. E.

ORDERLY. Fall in, men, for company drill. (*the men fall in, in one rank across the stage ; on left of company, six men, including* CARL, *with equipments awkwardly put on*) Sergeant Simmons, take charge of the recruits!

BEN. All right, sergeant! (*goes up and looks at them with great care, adjusting their equipments, etc., until the company is marched off.*)

ORDERLY. Attention, company! Right dress! Front! Order arms! Attention to Roll Call! (*calls roll*) Company, shoulder arms! Right face! Right shoulder shift arms! Forward! March!

[*Company exit,* R 3 E.

BEN. (*to recruits*). Come, fall in, here—and I'll see what I can do with you. Get into line here, somehow or other, can't ye? (*makes a line with butt of musket*) There, see if ye can toe that—now take the position of a soldier! Keep your heads up. (*all look up at the sky*) Ye darned fools! what are ye looking up there for? look to the front—spread out your toes more! (*they spread out their feet*) Keep your heels swag together. Say here! you there in the centre—why don't you carry yer gun as ye ought to ? (*recruit carries gun with barrel to the front, alters to some other position, but not the right one*) That's a goldarned nice way to hold a gun, ain't it ? Don't ye see how I hold mine ? (*they all hold their guns in different positions, some in left hand, etc.*) Hold yer barrels to the rear. (*they point their guns to the rear*) Darn yer skins, that ain't the way I mean. I mean the right way.

CARL. Is dot so, shargeant ?

BEN. (*at right of squad*. You dry up in the ranks. Right dress ! (*they arrange their coats*) What are you doing ? Look this way ! (*they leave the ranks to face him*) Git back, there! What in darnation do ye come out of the ranks for ? I mean turn your heads to the right. (*places them*) Front ! You, Dutchy, draw in your stomach !

CARL. Vat's dat ? You shust mind your own pizziness.

BEN. Ye gol darned chuckle head, why don't ye hold yer gun right ? Let me show you. (*moves for gun.*)

CARL. Vat's de matter mit you ? You vants mine gun ? You vas shust valk off of your ownself.

BEN. Let me show you how to hold it.

CARL. Nay, I shust keeps mine guns, if you bleases. You lafe me alone, or I shoots, und you vas got died. (*aims his gun at* BENNY.)

BEN. I'll have to give ye up. Now mind what ye are about. Right face ! (*some face right, others left*) Darnation, that ain't right. I never saw such doin's in all my life. Do ye know anything or don't ye ? (*they face about, trying to get into right position*) There, stand this way ? (*places them*) Now I want ye to look straight at me, and do jest as I do ! (*hesitates, scratches his head, after taking off his hat. All do the same*) Christopher Jerusha ! What are ye doin' ? (*throws his hat on the ground—all do the same*) Columbus Christopher ! (*brings down his gun ; all do the same, striking butts on their toes. They shout "oh,' and kick about.*)

CARL. Dunder and blitzen ! himmel, sturn, dunder vetter !

BEN. I'll be darned if I ain't about discouraged. Pick up your muskets and git into the ranks. Right face ! (*plac s them*) Right shoulder shift arms ! Not that way. Why don't you mind yer busiuess ? (*places muskets*) Forward, march ! Left, left, left, right, left. Change your step. Goldarn it, change your step. Left foot, left foot, now you've got it. Left, right, left, keep it, left, now you've got it, left, right, left, right foot, ye darned fool, ye lost it again, ye lost it again. Pick up your step, Dutchy.

CARL (*stoops and feels his foot*). I ish got mine step ; dat man vas crazy, sure !

BEN. (*kicks* CARL). Get out there, ye darned cabbage head ! (*all exit, R 3 E. Here can be introduced a bayonet or fancy drill, entering at double quick,* L. 3 E.)

SCENE II.—*Home of* WILD DAN *in Missouri.*

Enter DAN, MRS. SANFORD *and little* MARY.

DAN. Come, my darlings, come !

MRS. S. Oh ! it is so dreadful to be compelled to leave our home.

MARY. Papa, I don't want to go.

DAN. I know it, my darling, but we must go, they would kill you. The cowards would do it when I'm away.

MRS. S. We must, then, seek protection at the hands of the Northern people. So be it ! Come what may, Dan, I'll do as you bid me.

DAN. Your heart is in the right place, Mary. You are my own dear wife. Come, nestle, closer to me—so. How the past returns, now! I took you a bright, happy girl, and gave you but sorrow and misery.

MRS. S. Don't speak so.

MARY. No—you're my good papa.

DAN. Well—well! Come, come! Adieu, dear old home, adieu! Happy fireside, so often brightened by the smiles of those I loved best —good bye! good bye! We may never see you again. (*all exit,* L. 2. E.)

SCENE III.—*Wood, at night.*

Enter OLD REFUGEE, L 3 E., *with a staff, and staggering.*

OLD REFUGEE. Where can I hide? The blood-thirsty villains may kill me. Oh, God! I can't go any farther. (*falls*) Oh! for one hour of youth, that I might defend my home and wife from the bloodhounds. (*a light is reflected on scene, from a distance*) Heavens above! What is that light? (*rises on his elbows and looks*) It is a house on fire! Oh, God! they have set fire to my house! (*falls, weeping.*)

Enter CORPORAL SCRUBBS *and* DICK, L. 2 E.

SCRUBBS. Halloa! Old man! what are you doing down thar?

OLD REF. I'm faint, and cannot walk.

DICK (*calls* CORPORAL). Sh—! (CORPORAL *comes down.*)

OLD REF (*looks up and recognizes them and shudders*). Heavens! they will kill me.

DICK. I say, Corporal, that's the old man whose house we've just burned! I'll bet you he's got his money with him, and is going to join the Yanks.

SCRUBBS. Your head's level, Dick! Say, here old man! Got any money about you? Out with it.

OLD REF. Oh, sir! don't rob me.

SCRUBBS. Well, hand me the money, then; or I'll put a bullet through you, you dog-goned old nigger lover! (*they rifle his pockets.*)

OLD REF. (*trying to free himself*). Help! help!

DICK (*choking him*). Hush!

SCRUBBS. Let him take this! (*snaps pistol at him*) Darn the pistol! I never knew it to miss fire before.

OLD REF. For God's sake, don't kill me. I'm old and feeble, and I cannot live long; don't kill me! If you have a gray-haired father, don't shoot; by the memory of your mother, don't! For Heaven's sake don't kill a poor defenceless old man.

SCRUBBS (*strikes him on the head with butt of pistol*). There, shut up, you dog-goned old Yankee lover!

DAN (*outside*). Come along, I'll soon pilot you to a place of safety— come along!

DICK. Quick, some one is coming this way!

Enter DAN, MRS. SANFORD, *little* MARY, *and* REFUGEES, L. 2. E,

DAN (*see'ng* CORPORAL *and* DICK). Ha! stand back there. (SCRUBBS *escapes, as* DICK, *striking at* DAN *with knife, is shot by the scout.*)

Enter a squad of SOLDIERS, R. U. E.

SERGEANT OF SQUAD. Who fired that shot?

DAN. I did, Captain, I fired at that gray cuss, for waylaying this old man. (*to* OLD REFUGEE) Speak! who are you? Are you hurt badly?

OLD REF. (*feebly*). Yes! I cannot see. Who are you?

DAN. A friend.

OLD REF. I m dying. They came—murdered my wife because she loved the dear old flag—pillaged and burned my house. I alone escaped their fury. I was seeking protection in the Union lines, when I was waylaid. Don't leave me, I'm dying; they hunted me down, because I would not turn traitor! I die—I—I—God bless the Union. (*dies.*)

DAN (*places his hand on* REFUGEE'S *heart*). He is dead! But his death shall be avenged! (*feels flag in bosom of* OLD REFUGEE) But what is this! (*exhibits flag*) Brave heart, you have indeed died beneath the old flag. There, men, lies the body of a true American! old and feeble he was—but he remained true to his country! one of the noblest examples of loyalty and patriotism. Through the storms of life, and the dangers of the times—while neighbors and friends turned traitors, he loved the old flag and never forsook it. Sleep, brave heart, sleep! You've gone up there to get your reward. (*spreads flag on the body, all kneel around and lay hands on it, with heads uncovered*) And may He who watches over us all, take you to his care. and protect the dear old flag from the assaults of ambitious men!

●

Tableau: Moonlight over group!   Silent oath.

SCENE IV.—*A Street.*

Enter MEHITABLE, L.

MEHITABLE (*with letter in hand*). I'm so glad my Benny is well; and, then he tells me he's beating all the rebels.'

Enter DR. BOLUS, R., *and listens.*

I ought to be there to help him—oh! Lor'! wouldn't I scratch, though?

DR. BOLUS (*aside*). Rather peculiar girl, that. (*aloud*) How do you do, Miss Mehitable?

MEHIT. I don't do at all, sir. I'm going hum. (*going.*)

DR. B. Oh, dear no—(*aside*) she isn't bad-looking. (*aloud*) Mehitable —how's the folks at home?

MEHIT. The folks at hum? You might ask how's the folks in the war.

DR. B. But I was thinking of you, Mehitable; I always thought you were a smart girl.

MEHIT. Smart girl? Tell me something I don't know.

DR. B. (*aside*) Strategy is the essential point in love as in war; so, here goes. (*aloud*) I'm rich. Mehitable.

MEHIT. You don't say?

DR. B. I'm young yet.

MEHIT. And confoundedly ugly.

DR. B. (*aside*). Rather personal. (*aloud*) I'm single—and——

MEHIT. See, here, Mr. Impudence—I don't want you or any one like you—if you were a man, you'd leave off pretending you're a cripple, and go down South to fight the rebels—them's my sentiments.

DR. B. For the sake of argument, I grant you're right, Miss Pie Crust —for the sake of argument—mind. (*aside*) She's good looking.

MEHIT. Argument? There's Mr. Stewart who's all powerful set back because his daughter is going to leave for the war. Miss Alice herself tries to look gay. Everything is topsy-turvy—that's argument for you.

DR B. I am well aware of that.

MEHIT. Well, then, mind your business.

DR. B. I will—I'll go and see the Stewarts—and if they're in trouble, I'll pour oil on the troubled waters ; if they're in despair, I'll give balm to their wounded spirits. (*goes out at* L.)

MEHIT. Oil, water and barm—very queer things to cheer up a family's drooping spirits. [*Exits,* R.

SCENE V.—*Home of* ALICE STEWART. *Door and windows at back. Chairs, tables, etc.* ALICE *in travelling dress, and all characters of scene, except* HARRY *and* MEHITABLE, *discovered.*

Enter MEHITABLE, R. 2 E., *carrying boxes, etc.*

MEHITABLE. Oh, Miss Alice! I'm so upset—and so is your father—and so is all your friends, to think that you're going down South, to the war.

ALICE. Are you? I'm glad to learn somebody will miss me. Has Mr. Woodruff arrived ?

MEHIT. He sent word that he would be here soon. But, Miss Alice, mustn't Mr. Woodruff love you just a little wee bit, at least, to come that far for you ?

ALICE. You silly girl! Harry and I were schoolmates.

MEHIT. (*aside*). Then, Benny and I were schoolmates. (*aloud*) I hope no harm will come to you. [*Exit,* R.

Enter HARRY, *at back.*

ALICE. Harry !

HAR. Alice! (*they grasp hands.*)

ALICE. You see, I've not delayed—I'm ready.

HAR. It denotes an anxiety to go, which I cannot understand in one in your social position.

ALICE. I cannot better prove my devotion to the Union cause, and if I can but make one poor soldier's last hour comfortable, I shall feel that I have done something to be proud of.

HAR. I would much prefer that we never part again.

ALICE. We have missed you very much since you left with the regiment.

HAR. And *I* have missed *you* more than I could express. Before we part again, promise to be mine, Alice. I have loved you dearly—Alice, speak !

ALICE. I——

HAR. Say the word.

ALICE. Yes ! (HARRY *and* ALICE *retire up stage.*)

DR. B. I love to see the warriors leave for the field. I assure you, ladies and gentlemen, that were it not for the fact that I'm a cripple, I'd be in the field.

MR. W. In the cornfield, may be.

MR. S. No one doubts the Doctor's patriotism.

MR. W. Oh, no !

ALICE. Doctor, will you accompany us?

DR. B. If I was not a cripple, I——

MR. S. We fully understand your position, Doctor.

MR. W. That's easy. The weather's bad—down South.

Enter MEHITABLE, R.

MEHITABLE. Dr. Bolus, here's a letter for you.

DR. B. It's from my son in the army—there is news in it.

MEHIT. I think it's from Miss—I've forgotten her name.

MR. W. A lady, Doctor! Does she know you're a cripple?

DR. B. It's all a mistake—I have no lady correspondent. (*opens letter and reads apart.*)

MR. W. (*aside*). The Doctor ought to organize a company, and stay home rainy weather.

DR. B. It's from my son. He's turned sutler, and informs me he's made ten thousand dollars during last month. There's a patriot for you! That boy 'll be promoted to some very important command, yet. (*train whistle heard and cars seen through window and door at back.*)

HAR. The train is in—Good-bye. (*shakes hands with friends.*)

ALICE. Good-bye. (*to her father*) Don't be alarmed on my account—I will write to you very often.

MR. S. (*to* HARRY *and* ALICE). God bless you both. (*kisses* ALICE.)

MR. W. Good-bye! May God's protection accompany you.

[HARRY *and* ALICE *exit at back.*

DR. B. I wish I had a daughter to send, I'd send her in a minute.

MR. W. (*overhearing him*). Yes—but you wouldn't go yourself. Doctor—you're a fraud. (DR. BOLUS *runs about excitedly, then sits down exhausted.*)

Scene closes as villagers, etc., wave their handkerchiefs.

SCENE VI.—*A Wood.*

Enter REBEL SCOUT, L.

SCOUT. Curses on the luck that led my horse into that ravine! Only for that, I'd be within our lines before this. I must carry these papers all safe to the General, or it will go hard with me. If I should come across any Yanks, I don't know how I should get away from them. I must find another horse. [*Exit*, R.

Enter DAN, L.

DAN. My wife and little one are safe—and now I must proceed on my mission. I must secure those dispatches, or the whole army may be caught in a trap. I'm on somebody's trail—it can't be a Union man, for he's making for the rebel lines. If it should only prove to be that rebel scout. I did well to send his horse down that ravine. It has been a long chase—both our horses are dead, and we are evenly matched. Now, with God's help, I will have the papers [*Exit*, R.

SCENE VII.—*Landscape. Camp in the distance.*

Enter REBEL SCOUT, R. 3 E.

SCOUT Some one is following me. How can I throw him off the scent? (*shows papers*) These are safe, so far! (*hears noise* L.) Ha! some one comes this way. I must retrace my steps.

Turns to exit R *, when* DAN *enters*, R. 3 E.

DAN. Hold your hosses. (REBEL *draws knife and strikes at* DAN) You gray cuss, is that your game? (*they grapple.* DAN *seizes the knife, and points revolver at his head*) Make another move like that, and I'll put day-light clean through you. I want those papers you are carrying to Lee! Come, out with them.

SCOUT. You shall never have them. (*struggle.* DAN *secures papers.*)

REBEL SOLDIERS *enter at* L. 2 E. DAN *fires and kills a* REBEL ; *is then overpowered by* REBELS.

REBEL OFFICER (*takes papers from* DAN *and puts them in his bosom*). We've got you at last! Well, you won't live long to give us more trouble. Secure his hands, men! Take those pistols—off with his belt—search him—take that hat off. Dan Sanford, I'm going to shoot you like a dog! I know you! you have entered our camps at night, and stolen our plans. You have spied our movements—and baffled many an attempt to beat the cursed Yanks. You have but a few minutes to live. Speak, if you have anything to say.

DAN. I haven't got much to say. You know me, do you? But I know you better, for it was you and your confederates that drove my wife and child from their peaceful homes—but I am avenged, you cowards!

REBEL OFFICER. Bandage his eyes, men.

DAN. Stay! I have one request to make. You are going to murder me. I am ready to die. I only wish I could live long enough to defend the dear old flag from your traitorous blows. Fire! you cowards! but let me die as a brave man should—with unbandaged eyes,—looking toward that heaven where my sainted mother is watching me now.

REBEL OFFICER. Attention, men! Shoulder arms! ready! Kneel, Dan Sanford, and receive your just deserts.

DAN. There is but One, to whom I bow the knee. Fire! I fear you not.

REBEL OFFICER. Aim!

UNION SOLDIERS, *headed by* JACK WOODRUFF, *rush in,* R. 2 E. *They engage* REBELS. DAN *frees his hands.* REBELS *are overpowered.* DAN *knocks down* REBEL OFFICER—*takes papers from his bosom, and points revolver at his head. All form a beautiful picture.*

Tableau : " Emancipation."

ACT III.

SCENE I.—*Union Camp. Tents at back. Early morn.* TIM *and* CARL *discovered in same tent. Fire in centre. Kettle of water over it.*

TIM (*rises*). Phat time is it? I dunno. (*yawns*) Say, Dutchy, get up! (*tickles* CARL.)

CARL (*awaking*). Dunder, Teem, shtop dot!

TIM. Git up out o' dat. It's near reveille.

CARL (*rising*). If you don't late me alone, I vas put a plack eye py your nose. (*comes out of tent with basin, towel, and shirt.*)

TIM. Howld yer whist! Phat the divil are ye goin' to do?

CARL. Vash mine shirt.

TIM I guess I moight as well take a hand in it. Lay out yer howld o' that soap, Dutchy.

CARL. Vat you tinks I vas a jackasses?

TIM. Out, ye shcut, I want none o' yer palarvering.

CARL. Vat you say? I vas a scoot? I make you a stomach pain py your head.

TIM. See here, me good man—I'll have none o' yer blackguard capers wid me, an' if it wasn't for the dacency 1 howld for a sojer, an' the respect I have for a bigger man than meself, I'd knocks yer brains out aginst me brogue—do ye mind dat now?

Enter BENNY, R. U. E.

BEN. Here, O'Brien, it's darned near time you'd let Dutchy alone.

TIM *going up*. All right, Sergeant. (*goes up to fire.*)

CARL. You vas a pully man, Shargent.

BEN. Yours, truly. If he don't quit his darned nonsense, I'll put him in the guard-house.

CARL. Pully, pully, Shargent.

BEN. (*to* CARL). I'm kind o' sort o' hard up for fifty cents—let me have half a dollar till the paymaster comes 'round.

CARL. You—you vash a nice peebles. (*hands the money.*)

BEN. Yours, truly. That's all hunky. Dutchy, I've got a bran new knife—don't you want to swop? It's an all-fired good one. It comes from Germany.

CARL. Is dot so? Vat's dot swoppy fellow?

BEN. I'll swop it for shin-plasters. Look at it. It's jest as sharp as a razor.

CARL (*after looking at knife*). Dot knife vas irons.

BEN. Wall, I swan, if you ain't the darndest queerest critter I ever see. It's o' the best steel ever made. It'll cut a har jest as quick as butter. Let me have one of yer har.

CARL. Dunder und blitzen! Vat for you do dot? I gets as mad as der dyvel——

BEN. Wall, I'll tell you, Dutchy. Give me two dollars for it—and I'll call it square.

CARL. Dot vas doo mooch.

BEN. Give me a dollar for it, and I'll give you double rations to boot.

CARL (*hands money*). Dot knife vas Yerman! I give you von dollar, not so much py fifty cents.

BEN. Yours, truly. Fork it over (*aside*) The darned old knife wa'n't worth a cent. (*aloud*) All right, Dutchy—I'll see you again.

[*Exit*, R. U. E.

CARL. I vos got dem vash tings und soaps all by mine own self, now. (*during the above*, TIM *has filled the basin with boiling water instead of the cold water* CARL *had in there.*)

TIM (*aside*). Be jabers, I'll be avin wid ye, me boy.

CARL. Mine Gott! I vears dot shirt only six months, und I guess id dake six months to clean vash him. (*puts his hands into water*) Oh! Sacremento! Donner-vetter! Dunder und blitzen!

TIM. Oh! worra, worra, Dutchy, phat's the matter?

CARL. You vas a shwindle peeples—a humpug Irishmens! (*they grapple.*)

Enter DAN, L. U. E.

DAN. Hold your hosses! Get out o' here!

TIM *and* CARL *run out*, L., *as* GENERAL *enters*, R. 2 E. DAN *salutes* OFFICER, *and presents pass.*

GENERAL. You are the man I've been expecting. What success has attended your efforts?

DAN. Rather of an encouraging nature, General. May I speak here?

GEN. Yes.

DAN. A few days ago, I came across a rebel scout, who, I had reason to believe, carried important dispatches.

GEN. To whom?

DAN. General Lee. After a struggle, I secured the papers. Here they are.

GEN. (*after reading*). Good! Oh! oh! reinforcements for Lee. Young man, this will be of great service to the Commanding General. You deserve promotion—and I will see that——

DAN. General, I am much obliged to you, but I'd rather serve as a private soldier. As such, I can do more valuable service than I could as a commissioned officer.

GEN. You are very modest, but have it as you will, at present. I'll remember you. I must leave you now. The enemy camped in force on our right last night, and we may be attacked at any moment. I must proceed to headquarters.

DAN. One moment, General, if you please. Like you, I noticed, last night large fires on your right, and surmised that the enemy was there in force. While endeavoring to get through their lines, I found myself accidently in their midst. They had no fires, everything was still—and this was on your left. Rather surprised, I began to reconnoitre and satisfied myself that the noise proceeded from empty wagons, and the fires you saw were kindled purposely to deceive you. The whole force of the enemy is massed on your left, and a flank movement is no doubt intended on the Union line.

GEN. (*grasps his hand*). Noble fellow! Better and better! You may have saved us from total defeat. Here, come over to my tent and rest yourself; I'll at once to headquarters, for our forces must be moving on them immediately.

DAN (*taking off his gray disguise*). Thank you, General, I await your further orders. How good it is to feel once more the Union blue. It makes one feel like a new man. (*reveille sounds, as* DAN *and* GENERAL *exit at* R. U. E., *and scene closes.*)

SCENE II.—*Picket Line.*

CARL *on picket enters,* L. U. E. *Rain falling*

CARL. Dis vorld vas full of drooblos py me! Dese American peeples vas fight like der dyvel. Of mine Yerman gountry—I vas Yerman, oh! yaw!—of mine gountry I vas a pully habby poy fon my mudder. She vas a pully vomans—oh, yaw! Ven I vas lefe mine Yerman gountry, I come py New York. Ven I come py dot places—dot Kaystal gartens— a man come py me, und dot mans says: "How you vas, Carl?" Mine Gott, I don't know dot mans, but dot mans knows mine fatter, mine mudder; und all mine peeples of mine Yerman gountry. Ve have swei lager —und goot dinners. Dunder! dot man's vos gone py me—und I find myself py der mood gutter—und my pockets vas turned inside owit—und my monish vas gone, py cracious! I moost look owit fur de repels. (*shot heard, he dodges*) Mine Gott in himmel, dem repels vas shoot loose und careless! Der rain vas bade fur soldier poys vat vas on bicket. (*sings In the representation the 2d and 3 l verses may be omitted.*)

Oh! der rain, der putiful rain,
Sblashing der ground mit a big wet shdain,
Shdopping de drop on a fair lady's nose,
Indo de soles of your boods id goes.
        Sblashing,
                Dropping,
                        Bouring so gay,
As id fasd drobs down, mosd efery vet day.

Oh! der putiful rain, so damp,
Vet enough do gafe you a gramp;
How nice id sooks you droo your glothes
(Id blays der very doose mid dose),
        Vedding,
                Shboiling,
                        Soaging droo,
Der putiful rain vad shdrikes righd droo.

Thunder and lightning.   Scare of CARL, *who, after a moment, resumes.*

See der vild crowd as id scoods along,
Calling each oder, mit gurse loud und shdrong,
As id shdrikes ouds ids legs, each one does him shdrain
Do god oud der vay of der putiful rain,
        Running,
                Flying,
                        Scooding aboud,
Und gursing der putiful rain no doubd.

Vonce I vas vet like der rain so free,
Bud now I am alvays so try as gan be;
Like der rain, as in bunches der cround id toes peat,
I ofden have laid me all over de schdreed,
        Dumbling,
                Drolling,
                        Rolling aroundt,
Somedimes in der gudder I rolled from der ground.

(*rustling heard among the leaves*) Vat's dot?—py cracious—dem vas peen repels, sure. Oh! mine Gott! mine Gott! You shust valk off of your ownself—look oud—I shoots. (*fires at back.*)

Enter JEFF, *who falls, kicks about, and yells.*

Scene closes.

SCENE III.—*A Wood.*

Enter RICHMOND, *followed by a* SOLDIER, L.

RICHMOND. Go and learn whether Corporal Scrubbs has returned. If he has, tell him I await him here.   [*Exit* SOLDIER, R.
How glad I am that it is day!—it gives me a short respite to the hideous visions that haunt me in my sleep. For nearly three long years has my breast been torn by conflicting emotions—until scarce one ray of hope is left! My early aspirations—all—all—shattered—and what have I realized? Military honor! But at what price? The devastation of my

native State—the sacrifice of my first, my only love! (*pause*) Ah! Alice! Alice! there was a time when, but for one sweet smile, I would have been your slave—your very dog. But now—now—that my devotion is scorned—the love I bore you is turned to hate—to fiendish hate—even as my smiling native fields are turned to charred and blackened desolation. Should we ever meet again, you will find me changed indeed! God help me! there are times when, if I had you in my power——

Enter CORPORAL SCRUBBS, R.

Well, Corporal, what report?

SCRUBBS (*dressed in blue*). I have seen her.

RICH. Then she is with the army?

SCRUBBS. A nurse.

RICH. You are positive?

SCRUBBS. The very description you gave me.

RICH. Did you learn her name?

SCRUBBS. Alice! I heard it pronounced by a young man in a lieutenant's uniform.

RICH. Then come, bright day which sees the accomplishment of my revenge!

SCRUBBS. You would not kill her, Captain?

RICH. Why not?

SCRUBBS. She is a woman, and——

RICH. (*seizes his arm*). Fool! I do not kill those whom I love, unless they are too stubborn in their refusals. (*blows whistle*)

Enter REBELS, L.

Men, I have a detail for you to-day. It will take us, perhaps, from the main main army, and I will have a special duty for you to perform. May I count on you? Even to seize and carry away a woman?

SOLDIERS. Yes, yes. Three cheers for the Captain!

RICH. Then follow the Corporal. I will be with you in a moment.

[*Exit* SOLDIERS *and* SCRUBBS, L.

(*following*) And, now, fate beckons me to happiness or misery. But, come what may, I will not rest until at least I have revenge. [*Exit*, L.

SCENE IV.—*A Wood. Battle of The Wilderness.*

Drums and bugles sound. Firing heard at a distance. Union Skirmishers advance and retreat. Enter Regiment with colors. HARRY WOODRUFF *at the head of color-company. Regiment fires and charges across the stage —is repulsed, and* REBELS *advance with a yell. Enter* RICHMOND, L.

RICHMOND. The day is ours, so far. Now, let the cursed Yankees be exterminated. (*commands*) Forward, men.

Enter second line of REBELS.

Halt! Lay down. The cursed Yankees are driving our men back. (*first line come back on the fly, going over second line. When clear, orders*) Ready! aim! fire! Attention! Repel charge! (RICHMOND *urges his men on. Union troops enter, and charge. the color-bearer is seen to fall.* HARRY *seizes the colors and rushes on.* RICHMOND *seizes Union colors. During the struggle—*RICHMOND *is knocked down by* CAPTAIN JACK WOODRUFF, *who, in turn, is shot down.* TIM *is also seen falling, wounded in the foot.* REBEL *flag torn down. The Union banner triumphant !*

Tableau—Curtain.

ACT IV.

SCENE I.—*Battlefield at Midnight.*

Moonlight. Dead and wounded lying about. Among the latter, are discovered RICHMOND, *suffering from the stunning blow received in the ba tle, and* TIM, *wounded in the foot. Stage filled with war debris, i. e., guns, muskets, etc., left in previous scene.*

TIM (*rising on his elbows*). Ough! This was the divil's own day's work. Faith, an' I would not go over it again for a place on the New York police force. Ough! what a night! It's not well I'm feeling with this hole in my foot. I feel quite wake, too. The divil a bit to ate have I had at all, at all, since yisterday. Bad luck to the Johnnies, any way. (RICHMOND *groans*) Sh—who is that? Be the powers o' war, it's that same fellow, Magruder, who used to be after Miss Stewart.

RICH. Drink! Drink!

TIM. Is it water ye want? Thin ye shall have some if Tim O'Brien's got it. (*finds his canteen empty*) Not a dhrop! But I'll find you some. (*attempts to rise*) Oh! God. (*falls exhausted.*)

RICH. (*raising himself*). Oh, for a drop of cold water to quench my thirst! What has weakened me so? I am not wounded. Oh, my head! it was that fearful blow! Water! Water!—but not from a cursed Yankee. (*sees* TIM) Ha! this man!—oh! my recollections! Where have I seen him? To-day, in the fight? I know him now. But oh! he shall not leave this field alive. Dog, I will kill you! (*draws knife from his belt and crawls to* TIM. *Just as he is about to strike,* TIM, *who has noticed his approach and divined his purpose, stops his arm, wrenches knife from him, and is about to strike him dead.*)

TIM. No—I will not kill ye. It would only be sending ye to the divil, for nobody but his cloven-footed majesty would have the likes of ye. Kape still, ye blackguard, or I'll do it yet. It's a moighty fine thing for ye that I'm an Irish gintleman from the county o' Cork, or, be the howly St. Patrick, it's purty quick you'd have to start for Ould Nick's pepper garden. Be aisy, now. (*rises, takes a gun for a crutch, and starts with canteen for water.*)   [*Exit at* R. 2 E.

RICH. What! is there no water about here? (*crawls up to right of field, picks up a canteen of water and drinks*) Oh! how refreshing it is! Now for safety! If I remain here, the Yankees will pick me up.

Enter REBEL SOLDIERS, L. 2 E., *with lanterns and stretcher, in search of* MAGRUDER, *headed by* SCRUBBS.

At last, friends are near.

SCRUBBS. This way, Captain, we've been looking for you.

Enter ALICE *and other* NURSES *at* R. U. E.

RICH. (*aside*). What do I see? The Union nurses! Alice must be

one of them. Now for my purpose ; but I am too weak. Curses on it.
Ah ! they will do it for me. (*lies on the field and signs to* REBELS *to crouch
in the dark.* ALICE *comes down to* RICHMOND *and stops, while the other*
NURSES *attend to other wounded, and exit, gradually, at* R. *and* L.)

ALICE. This man breathes. He wears the gray. But what matters it,
true charity should make no discrimination with the blue and the gray
dying and wounded. Drink of this, my good man ? (*recognizes him*)
Richmond Magruder ! you here, and wounded ! I will call for assistance, and have you taken to the hospital. Oh, sir. Do not refuse it.

RICH. (*rising*). I do, for I do not need it. Here, to-night, beneath
Heaven's moonlight—with the groans of dying men in my ears—I ask
you, Alice Stewart—have you forgotten who I am ?

ALICE (*coldly*). Sir, I came to assist some of the wounded braves, who
fell in to-day's fierce battle—and not to tell you whether I have forgotten you or not. (*turns to leave.*)

RICH But you shall not leave me. Here, in the very teeth of your
watch hounds, I will have you. Here, men ! (REBEL SOLDIERS *seize*
ALICE, *and stop her cries*) Take her away !

Enter CARL *and* TIM, R. 2 E. ; *both, guessing the situation, engage* REBELS,
but are overpowered.

RICH. Quick ! quick ! Men, to camp with her. I'll follow you. (*to
men over* CARL *and* TIM) You, men, bring those two scoundrels along.
                    [*Exit* SCRUBBS *and* SOLDIERS *with* ALICE, L. 3 E.
Ha ! ha ! ha ! Dogs, I am not baffled yet.   [*Exit*, L. 3 E.

TIM. Ah ! ye durty blackguards—if ever I catch ye in New York, I'll
make a holy show of ye. Let go yer howld on me—do ye hear—let go.
(*struggles.*)

                    Enter BENNY, R. 2 E.

BENNY. What is all this about ? Ah ! (*knocks down one of the* REBELS.
CARL *frees himself from the other, and* REBELS *are overpowered. To* REBEL
down) Yours, tru—nary a time.

CARL. Yaw. Yours, tru—by you too—nary a dime ! (NURSES *reap-
pear.*)

                    Tableau.

SCENE II.—*A Wood.*

Enter DAN *at* L., *hurriedly.*

DAN. Where are they taking that woman to ? She must be a prisoner,
and in the hands of Richmond Magruder. By heavens, she can't stay
there—but they're too many for me just at present. It would be fool-
hardy in me to attempt the rescue now. But I know where his camp
lies, and I'll return. Now for some assistance.

Enter HARRY, R.

Ah ! some one comes ! (*to* HARRY) Say, Captain, I want your help.

HAR. For what ?

DAN. To rescue a woman from a gang of rebel cut-throats.

HAR. I'm willing. But what is it ? a love affair ? We soldiers don't
meddle much in such matters.

DAN. Love affair to the deuce. It's an affair of honor. I'm a soldier as well as you. (*opens coat and shows blue blouse*) My name is Dan Sanford, and my business——

HAR. A scout. I have heard very favorably of you.

DAN. Then, listen. Just now, I saw a young lady forcibly carried off by rebels—Richmond Magruder and his gang.

HAR. (*starts*). Magruder!

DAN. Yes—do you know him?

HAR. Slightly. Go on. The girl, who is she?

DAN. That I don't know.

HAR. (*excitedly*). Was she tall?

DAN. Yes.

HAR. (*with increasing excitement*). Did she wear the dress of a hospital nurse?

DAN. Yes.

HAR. Heavens! it is Alice!

DAN. You know her?

HAR. Do I know her? Young man, just now you asked me to assist you in her rescue—why, I would give my life to save her.

DAN (*aside*). I guess the lover is on his side. (*to* HARRY) Then return to camp. Bring along two or three men, and meet me at daybreak near the brick house on the turnpike, back of the cornfield.

HAR. I will. Thanks, thanks. Oh! Alice—Grant, Heaven, we may not be too late.   [*Exit*, R.

DAN (*going* L.). I guess he means business. Now, Magruder, look out for yourself.   [*Exit*, L.

SCENE III.—*Prison pen in Saulisbury, N. C. Stockade, and guard walking his beat; dead line near stockade at back. Prisoners lying about.* CAPT. GREY *at back*—CAPT. JACK WOODRUFF *in centre. Sun rising.*

Enter REBEL SERGEANT, L. U. E.

REBEL SERGEANT. Come, get over into line there, if you want your rations. [*Exit with the prisoners, at* L. U. E., *except* CAPTS. GREY *and* WOODRUFF.

CAPT. WOODRUFF (*looking after comrades*). I can't go—I'm too weak—and it makes but little difference. Oh, God! must there be men so devoid of manliness as to starve those they fear to fight? Another weary night has passed and brought another day—but no food, no shelter—it has brought with it naught but daylight to see *our* misery in our comrades' faces—wakefulness to feel our woes and appreciate the price of patriotism. Oh! this hunger—how costly this devotion! Lank and lean, cold and dying for want of bread and warmth. My comrades will have bread—they can still turn out; but soon the pittance will prove as insufficient for them as it has for me. The detail is coming this way. Bread—bread!

Enter REBEL SERGEANT *and* SOLDIER, *carrying pail,* L. U. E.

REB SERGEANT. Shut up, you dog-goned Yankee—shut up. (*kicks him*) Do you want bread? I'll tell you how you can get bread, meat, and everything you want.

CAPT. W. (*partly rising*). Oh! say—how—you're good—you would not see me die——

REB. SERGEANT (*shows him meat and bread*). Here is meat and bread!

CAPTAIN W. (*seizing the food*). Oh! give it to me!

Reb. Sergeant. You can have this, and more too. Join the Confederate army, and you can have all the food and clothing you want.

Captain W. Is that your condition?

Reb. Sergeant. It is.

Captain W. (*throwing down food*). Take your food—I would rather starve a thousand times than turn traitor to my country.

Reb. Sergeant (*returns meat to the pail, and throws down a crust of bread*). Then take that, and stop your noise, or I'll put a bullet through you. [*Exit*, L. U. E.

Captain W. (*eating*). How good this bread is—if I only had more of it.

Captain G. (*groans*). Bread! Bread! I'm hungry—bread!

Captain W. What, a comrade without bread, while I'm eating? No —it shall not be! Yet, I'm so hungry. I—but——

Captain G. I'm dying! Bread!

Captain W. Here, take my bread, captain—if we go hungry together, we can feast together, though we have but a crust to feast on. How quick the ration goes and only leaves a reminder of the conquering hunger—oh, God! in this dread respite is there no permanent relief? Hast thou brought with this day no ray of hope, no comforter? and is the trial still to hold out? The sun! God has sent the sunlight through the thick, dark, death-brooding branches! Oh! the time was when the sunlight shone on my life—happy days! youthful aspirations! Loves! a mother's caresses and tender care—a dear and kind father. How well I remember their counsels, guiding me onward on the road of life. Then, a dear wife and beloved children—the dear little flaxen-haired darlings, how well I can see the sunlight pouring in on their heads while they made home happy with their innocent prattlings! oh! I yearn to see them. Will I ever behold their dear faces again? Would they know me now with glassy eyes, livid lips and sunken cheeks? Oh, God! must I die without clasping them to my heart once more? (*falls. Tableau: "Home." After Tableau*) I must warm myself in the sun. I cannot walk —my feet are numbed. (*crawls up in the sunshine.*)

Rebel Guard. Get back there, you dog-goned Yankee, get back, or I'll shoot you.

Captain W. The dead line, I forgot. Don't, I only wish to warm myself.

Reb. Guard. I'll warm you. (*fires.*)

Captain W. (*falls*). God! I'm shot.

Enter Prisoners, *who gather around him, from* L. U. E.

Captain G. Are you hurt, Captain?

Captain W. Yes, I'm dying—here—I'm shot. My wife, children! Comrades! (*wanders*) There, there, see, they come! Give me a musket. Boys, meet them like men—meet the traitorous knaves! Steady! Forward! March! Charge! Ha! sword to sword—breast to breast— mow them down as you would curs—meet them down the hill yonder— see! there are more of them! Stand your ground, boys! hand to hand! blow for blow! They waver! they give way! They're beaten! Huzzah! huz——(*dies.*)

Tableau: "Crowning of the American Soldier."

SCENE IV.—*A Wood.*

Enter Jeff, L.

Jeff. Gorry mity! but dis am tough work for a cullud pusson of my pedigree. Dis 'ere fighting, charging, rip and tare, am more than I bargained for. But I is no mean plantation nigger—I kin fight. Yes, let dem fellahs put me in de field and I'll strike for me altars and mo sires.

Enter BENNY, R.

BENNY. What on 'arth ails ye? Got a fit? You make more noise than a healthy tom-cat. How was it you skedaddled from the fight yesterday?

JEFF. Me, run away? no, sah! I was 'tacked by superior numbers. De rebels cut me short in my stragetic movements, and I was forced to retreat, but not afore I had cut dem down to pieces.

BEN. You don't say?

JEFF. Yes, sah. I rallied my corporosity to repel de 'vancing columns. De shock was awful—but de rebels soon found out what stuff I was made of, and started for home on a running double quick march. Dere was no loss on our side. De cullud troops fought bravely.

BEN. Well, I swan, you're entitled to promotion.

JEFF. Yes, sah, and I is gwine to be made an ossifer.

BEN. You were in a squeezing fix.

JEFF. Dat's so—but I's been in a tighter place 'fore.

BEN. When was that?

JEFF. Dat was when I was wagin driber. I had a load of powder, and was gwine 'long, when a shell from de rebels came and struck de wagin, an' 'sploded all de powder and blowed de hosses an' wagin into a thousand pieces.

BEN. How happened it you escaped?

JEFF. Oh, when I saw de shell strike an' de powder begin to burn, I—I—got off.

BEN. Jerusha! Jeff, you're powerful on the yarn. (*noise heard*) Halloa, what is that?

Enter CARL, *running*, L.

CARL. Shargeant, shargeant, dot gal vos peen daken avay py de repels.

BEN. What gal?

CARL. Dot gal vat dooks care of de wounded soldiers, dot gal vat vos peen carried avay ven you comes py repels und Teem und me.

BEN. I didn't see any gal carried off—you've been drinking sutler's cider.

CARL. So help mine coodness, shargeant, I——

BEN. Well, what gal?

CARL. Dot gal vat you call Miss Shtewart.

BEN. By the 'tarnal, you don't mean Alice Stewart?

CARL. Dot vas peen her.

BEN. Then why do you stand there for? Come, let us go to the general—and get some men Come.

Enter DAN, R.

DAN. Hold your hosses. I overheard you—don't go to the general, but get some of the boys, and meet me as soon as you can—don't delay, near the brick house, down the turnpike, back of the cornfield.

BEN. (*shaking him by the hand*). Yours, truly. If you had dropped from heaven, you might look a little more gentle, but you wouldn't be a darn bit more welcome. But your name?

DAN. Dan Sanford.

BEN. Oh! oh! (*aside to* CARL) That's Wild Dan, the scout; he's a good 'un. (*to* DAN) Young man, yours—yours, truly. (*going* R.) At the brick house—back of the cornfield?

DAN (*going* L.). At the brick house, back of the cornfield.

[*Exit* BENNY, CARL, *and* JEFF, R., DAN L.

SCENE V.—*Rebel Camp, at the foot of a mountain. At back, mountain with pathway at* L., *and a precipice,* R. *Tent at* R. U. E. *Sentries heard challenging.* RICHMOND *discovered in tent. When challenges have ceased,* RICHMOND *comes out of tent. Union flag (a trophy) seen in tent.*

RICHMOND. I slept but a while, yet what horrid dreams filled my soul. I went through battles—heard the rattle of the musketry, the roar of the cannon, and the groans and shrieks of the dying—saw the clashing sabres' flying sparks blind the combatants, friends fall—and behind the clearing smoke of battle, the enemy charging our line and mowing our men like ripe wheat. I saw that, and more—a horrid vision the thought of which almost stills the beating of my heart. Amidst all the uproar of defeat and death, I thought I stood alone—invulnerable,—and a voice called out, Richmond Magruder, you die not the death of the brave; your end will be that of the outlaw! Oh! (*buries his head in his hands.*)

Enter SCRUBBS, R. U. E.

SCRUBBS. Captain!

RICH. Ah! is it you, Corporal?

SCRUBBS. Yes, Captain. You seem agitated—you need quiet.

RICH. I feel much refreshed after my short sleep. And the prisoner?

SCRUBBS. She is surprisingly cool and collected, and desires to speak with you.

RICH. Changed her mind, eh? Well, conduct her hither. Station yourself near by, and allow no one to approach this place.

SCRUBBS. All right, Captain. [*Exit,* R. U. E.

RICH. So, so. I shall meet her again. But what will it bring? Love? Alas! she feels but little of that for me. Oh, what would I not have given once for her affection? for I loved her, aye, love her still.

Enter ALICE *with* SCRUBBS *at* R. U. E. *As* ALICE *enters,* DAN *appears behind tent. Exit* SCRUBBS, R. U. E.

DAN. Now for rescue! (*disappears behind tent.*)

RICH. (*going to* ALICE). Well, Miss Stewart, you wish to speak with me?

ALICE (*coldly*). Yes!

RICH. I suppose you wish to ask for your liberation.

ALICE. I demand simply what is justly mine—that you allow me to return to my friends.

RICH. And if I refuse?

ALICE. You cannot refuse. Oh, sir! there must be some lingering spark of manhood in your breast. You cannot have forgotten that you have a mother—a sister, perhaps—and thinking of them and of Heaven's stern judgment, you cannot, oh! you will not detain me any longer.

RICH. Yet, I fail to see why, having gone to the trouble of bringing you hither, I should allow you to depart now. Motives like mine do not vanish like air.

ALICE (*kneeling*). But, oh, sir! think,—you cannot carry this persecution any further. A poor, weak, motherless girl implores you for her liberty; let me go, and I will depart blessing you—and some day, whenever your lot of sorrows burdens you, the thought of this one good action will be like bright sunlight amidst the shadows of your sufferings. Oh, sir, do not, do not keep me here any longer.

RICH. (*aside*). How beautiful she is! (*moves as if to catch her up in his arms.*)

ALICE (*jumping up*). Stand back, sir. I am not here to purchase my liberty.

RICH. Oh! but will you not listen to me? What is to me your presence if it brings no love? Have you not sometimes given a thought to the anguish which must gnaw at my heart? I, that have loved you with a devotion filling the almost boundless expanse of my soul. (*movement of* ALICE) Oh, stay. Answer me—will you not be mine? I will be your slave, and know nothing but to obey your simplest wishes. Do not turn from me. I may have committed ills great and numerous, but I am not lost to all sense of good. I have had to struggle against my inheritance of life's storms, and it has embittered me. Be mine—and I will love you with such a wealth of affection, that you will, at least, esteem and respect me. I will be your friend, to signal and avert darkly brooding storms—to strangle foul calumny in its birth. I will love you, not as the idle, gilded degraded toy, but as the true, spotless woman who gave me her name. Your griefs I will share, and I will so lighten, by incessant love and kindness, your home's work and cares, that your life will be ever as the morn's refreshed waking. (*kneels*) Alice! (*attempts to take her hand*) Alice!

ALICE (*moving from him*). Enough, sir!

RICH. (*aside, still kneeling*). Oh! (*aloud*) Stay! listen to me. Believe my love, undying——

ALICE (*going* R.). Love! As if it could exist in a villain's heart.

RICH. (*seizes her arm, turning her to left again*). Enough of mawkish sentiment. Remain there, and let us not mince matters, now. You have, by your hatred, goaded me almost to despair, and here I tell you, Alice Stewart, I hate you, but you shall be mine, or you leave not this place alive.

ALICE. I despise your threats as much as I do your dissembling. I fear you not. Scoundrels of your class are but cowards.

RICH. (*draws dagger*). By Heaven! you shall pay for this! (*brings out flag*) See the cursed colors of the North! Thus do I trample them beneath my feet!

ALICE. Shame! traitor, to thus insult the memory of your fathers. Shame, coward. Before a woman, you can act the braggart—but before a man, you would sneak into retreat.

RICH. Then take this! (*strikes at her. Shots heard.* RICHMOND *stops and turns to listen*) What can this mean? Yankees coming this way?

ALICE. Yes! They are my friends! Liberty or death! (*snatches revolver from* RICHMOND's *belt, seizes flag and runs at back*) One movement, and I fire—I will be free, or die beneath the flag that never knew defeat.

RICH. (*crouches in fear, and blows whistle. Enter* REBEL SOLDIERS, L U. E. *One of them seizes* ALICE's *arm and wrestles pistol from her*). Now, you shall pay for your rashness! (*seizes her in his arms and exits,* L. U. E. *Drums heard.*)

Enter HARRY, DAN, BENNY *and* SOLDIERS, R. U. E. REBEL SOLDIERS *retreat;* SCRUBBS *drops and pretends to be dead.*

DAN. Quick, that way—secure him.

HARRY. This way, men, this way!

DAN. Now, merciful Heaven, let our prayers be heard and give us success. (*disappears at back among the rocks, while* RICHMOND *appears on the mountain, with* ALICE. RICHMOND *drags her down to near the front. In the meanwhile,* SCRUBBS *has risen and made good his escape.*)

RICH. Now, for my revenge. See, below, the precipice where death awaits you, if you refuse. Say you will be mine, or you die.

ALICE A thousand deaths rather than dishonor! (HARRY *appears at back, on mountain, with* SOLDIERS) Harry! Harry! Harry!

HARRY. Heavens! Quick. (SOLDIERS *level their muskets as if to fire.* RICHMO⋅D *points dagger at the breast of* ALICE.)

RICH. Fire, if you dare, and I'll bury this blade in her heart!

HARRY (*strikes up muzzle of muskets with his sword*). Stay! he will kill her!

DAN (*emerging from among the rocks, strikes* RICHMOND). Just in time!

RICH (*staggers*). Ha! Foiled, ye devils! (*throws himself down precipice.* ALICE *is received in the arms of* HARRY.)

DAN (*looking over precipice*). Hold your hosses—I guess your goose is cooked this time.

BEN. (*seizing* DAN's *hand*). Yours, truly.

Tableau: Red Lights.

ACT V.

SCENE I.—*A Highway.*

BUMMERS, *led by* BENNY, *enter at* L. U. E. *They carry fowls, vegetables, etc.*

BENNY. Halt! ye darned cusses. Let's rest here. Our skirmishing for hen-coops and duck-ponds entitles us to a rest. (*looking off*) Keep shady; here comes one of the chivalry.

Enter CLERGYMAN, *with carpet bag*, L. U. E.

Hold on there, stranger; where are you going?

CLERGYMAN. I am going to preach in the next village. Pray let me pass.

BEN. What have you got in that bag? (CLERGYMAN *tries to escape*) No use, my Christian friend—we're going to know what you carry in there.

CLERGYMAN. I am a clergyman, gentlemen, on a peaceful mission. Pray do not detain me.

BEN. It don't make any difference what your mission is, we are going to dig into the vitals of your travelling companion to see what its robust corporosity contains; in vulgar language, we're going to see what you've got in that bag! (*wrests it from him.*)

CLERGYMAN. Please do not take my sermon, for I have to preach to-night. I assure you, that within that antiquated and very serviceable friend, nothing that the most covetous could long for, can be found. It contains but——

BEN. Draw in your breath, stranger; you can have your bag presently. (*has opened bag and pulls out long linen duster. Hands it to a* BUMMER, *who puts it on*) That's his surplice, ain't it, boys? (*takes out black bottle*) Halloa! here is his sermon. Let's see what the text is. (*reads label on bottle*) Old Rye Whiskey! That's a gol-darned good text, if the sermon will only go around. I've read its text, now for the perusal of its contents.

(*drinks, and passes it to* Bummers) Peruse, boys.   Pretty fiery sermon. (*smacks his lips*) It generally has a powerful effect on a congregation. (*pulls out an old white hat*) That's his chapeau. (*takes out a pack of cards*) Darn my buttons, but here's his credentials.   How are you, clergyman ? (*general laugh.*)

CLERGYMAN I beg of you, desist. You have robbed me of my medicine, and I shall suffer in consequence. Besides, I have an appointment.

BEN. Here is your bag, and here's the cover to your sermon, which was excellent. Good-bye, friend—yours, truly. (CLERGYMAN *going,* L.) Say, you long-winded cuss—you can fill out another sermon from the same text,—the subject ain't exhausted by any means. (*Exit* CLERGYMAN, R. U. E.) Well, boys, that fellah must be one of the hard-shell Baptists you read about. Darn my buttons, but his sermon was red hot. Halloa, here's another of them preachers.

Enter REV. AMASA GOODKIND, L. U. E.

How are you, old Gospel dispensary?

GOODKIND. Good day, gentlemen—I am weak, (*shows signs of exhaustion*) and really glad to meet you.   My son is somewhere in this vicinity, wounded and being cared for by some good colored people—and I have been searching for him until I am faint. (*about to fall.*)

BEN. (*steadying him*). Stand up—don't you go a-swooning around here —sofas are too scarce. (*aside*) I guess he wants a drink. (*aloud*) Here's something that'll put life into you. (*handing bottle.*)

GOOD. What is in this bottle ?

BEN. Don't be so darned pertik'lar—but drink. It's whiskey.

GOOD. (*handing back bottle*). No, gentlemen, no. Take back your poison —though I am weak and faint, I will not drink your rum.

BEN. Halloa ! what's the matter with you ? Who are you ?

GOOD. I am a minister of the Gospel, (BUMMERS *drop their bags, and gather around him gradually*) and a member of the commission sent out from Massachusetts to assist and give comforts to the brave defenders of the Union.   I was engaged in such duties when I heard of my poor boy, and am now in search of him, that I may press him to my heart, ere, perhaps, his soul takes its flight to Him who created it

BEN. Boys, fall in here—and help him along. (*to* GOODKIND) Then, you practice what you preach ?

GOOD. With God's help I try to do so.

BEN. And you won't drink ?

GOOD. No, gentlemen, no.   I must decline, though your offer is freighted with so much kindness.

BEN. Friend, (*grasping his hand*) yours, truly.   Excuse us—we're rough—and not used to meetin' men like you very often—but I guess none of us have yet forgotten the counsels we have received from our good mothers.

GOOD. I know it.

BEN. Here, boys, some water ! (*a* BUMMER *hands canteen and* GOODKIND *drinks*) It ain't often we get a chance to show that our hearts are in the right place, in religious matters ; but when it offers itself we're always ready to prove, that while we may be rough and don't have much gentility about us, we can tell the difference between a bogus Christian and one of the genuine kind, and we don't forget that we were once taught that God is our Master, and to practice charity. So cheer up. Here, boys, take this good man to camp (*two* BUMMERS *support* GOODKIND) and give him something to eat.   I guess the Kernel 'll take care of him.

GOOD. Thank you,   [*Exit,* R. U. E., *with two* BUMMERS.

Ben. Now, boys, let us move on.

Enter Corporal Scrubbs *and* Rebel Soldiers, l. u. e.

Scrubbs. Halt, there—down with those chickens. (Soldiers *cover* Bummers *with their muskets.*)

Ben. Eh! oh! why, boys, what's the use of makin' a fuss—sit down here and have something to eat and to drink. Why, we'll share with you —won't we, boys? (*winking at them.*)

Bummers. Yes, yes. Certainly!

Scrubbs. Well, seeing that you're friendly—we don't mind if we take a sup with you. Do we, boys?

Rebels. No, no, certainly not.

Ben. Well, come along, and sit down here. (Rebels *stand their muskets against trees, etc., and sit with* Bummers) Pass our sermon, boys. (*handing bottle around*) Peruse, gentlemen, peruse—our sermon is most instructive. (*whispers to nearest* Bummer, *who gets up, while the attention of the* Rebels *is drawn away from their muskets, and pours the water from his canteen into the barrels of the latter, then resumes his seat quietly.* Benny *jumps up, pistol in hand*) Now, my esteemed secesh cusses—pick up those bags.

Scrubbs and Rebels (*jumping up and seizing their muskets*). Betray'd! Down with the Yanks!

Ben. (*to* Bummers, *who have drawn their pistols*). Now, boys, when I give the signal pepper 'em. (*to* Rebels, *who have ineffectually snapped their arms*) No use, you gray cusses. you can snap but you can't bite. You read our sermon, but you couldn't see the point. So pick up those bags and go ahead of us. Now, boys, ready! aim! (Rebels *pick up bags, fowls, vegetables, etc., and walk ahead, followed by* Bummers *with aimed pistols*) That's the most effective preaching I've done in a long while.

[*All exit at* r. u. e.

SCENE II —*Camp of* Union Troops *on the march. Tents, camp-fires, etc.* Soldiers *lying here and there, some occupying themselves in chatting, others, in playing cards, etc. As scene opens, band heard discoursing "Hail Columbia."*

Enter Bummers *and* Rebels, r. 3 e.

Soldiers. Halloa!

Ben. Halt! (*to* Bummers) Now, boys, take those gray cusses down to the guard-house until I report to the Colonel, and I guess he'll find a place for them. (Rebels *unwilling to go*) Now, boys, ready! aim! (Rebels *march off and exit, at* l. 2 e.)

Carl. Say, Shargeant, you vas take dem repels—und they keep their guns—und don't shoot you?

Ben. Yes, they can't shoot with them muskets unless they put dry powder in them. I took care to have their barrels filled with water before they got occasion to use them against us. (*general laugh*) Well, Dutchy, darn yer buttons, we're goin' home. Ain't you glad?

Carl. Oh, mine coodness, I vas peen fine all over. I vants New York for sower-crout.

Ben. There, there, you are—greedy as ever; ye think of nothin' but eatin'.

Carl. Eating vas goot—don't you like eating?

Ben. When I'm hungry, certainly.

Carl. Vell, I vas peen hungry all der dimes.

BEN. I know it, darn ye. It's always the way with you—even when there's fighting to be did. Now, did you notice some time ago, how I got rid of that 'tarnal rebel who had carried away Alice Stewart—didn't I knock him down that mountain hole, and make him feel like a flattened pumpkin—didn't I?

CARL (*with surprise*). You vas schlop 'im on the copa!

BEN. Yes.

CARL. Nay—dot skrout vas peen de man.

BEN. Who?

CARL. Dot skrout mens—dot fellah vat vas peen vild as der dyvil.

BEN. You mean the scout, Wild Dan.

CARL. Yaw—dot vas de fellah.

BEN. Well, if he hadn't done it, I would. So it's all the same.

CARL. Oh! you vas too schmart. Say, Shargeant, I vas peen purty hard up. Lent me fumf zehn cents. I vas peen pay you all raight.

BEN. (*aside*). Oh! oh! (*aloud*) Well, Dutchy, I will, as soon as we are mustered out (*starts to go.*)

CARL (*stopping him*). Say, Shargeant, I vas hafe a fine knife from my Yerman gountry——

BEN. Oh, get out. (*runs out*, L. U. E.)

CARL. Dot mans vas humpug, sure. Vell, dis vorld vas peen full of droobles for me, any vay.

Enter HARRY *as a* COLONEL, L. U. E.

(*salutes*) Kernel, ve vas peen gone py dot blaco ve call homes. Eh?

HAR. Yes, my good man, the war is over. Lee and Johnston have surrendered, and our regiment is to be mustered out as soon as we reach Washington.

CARL. Is dot so?

HAR. Before we part, I have one duty to perform, and that is, to thank you, from the very bottom of my heart, for the part you took in the rescue of Miss Alice Stewart from the power of that bad man—Richmond Magruder.

CARL. Oh! Kurne, I vas only peen doing my duty as a man.

HAR. I know it. And not only in that instance, but throughout the war, have you and Tim O'Brien, by genuine devotion to your adopted country, thrown a never-fading lustre on the good name of the adopted sons of America, coming from your respective countries.

CARL (*overcome*). Mine Gott, Kurnel, I vas peen only a poor Deitch-man, but I'sh peen drue to dis gountry. And if dot repel Magruder vas peen not dead——

HAR. I heard that he still lives; but he will not attempt to injure me any more.

CARL. You petter look oud—he vas peen der dyvil, dot fellah——

HAR. Well, I forgive him!

Enter BENNY, L. U. E.

BENNY. Good morning, Kernel; when do we go to Washington, to be mustered out?

HAR. To-day, I think. But behave yourselves, boys; don't bring any disgrace on the regiment after going through the war in such gallant style.

BEN. Three cheers for Kernel Woodruff. (SOLDIERS *cheer*.)

HAR. Thank you, boys. I owe it all to your bavery. Thank you.

[*Exit, modestly*, R. U. E.

BEN. Boys, darn my skins, I'd like to be in the Kernel's place, when he gets home—he's going to get spliced.

CARL. Is dot so?

BEN. Yes, and to my cousin—the prettiest gal in the town. But never mind the girl and the splicin'—it makes a fellah feel queer about the heart. Dutchy, give us a song.

SOLDIERS. Yes, a song—a song.

CARL *sings.* *Afterwards scene closes as* SOLDIERS *cheer.*

SCENE III.—*A Street.*

Enter JEFF (*with portmanteau*), *dressed in civilian clothes,* L.

JEFF. Ough! Golly, dis am tough work. It's about time we got home—Kernel Woodruff would have to carry his own luggage, if we wasn't. Dis ere cullud gen'man's done gone got tired o' working, after fighting all fru de war. Golly, didn't I fight, though? (*going* R.)

Enter POMPEY, R., *also in civilian dress, running, knocks down* JEFF.

JEFF (*down*). Say, yere, you black nigger, what d'ye mean? (*rises.*)

POMPEY. What's de matter wid you, nigger?

JEFF. What for you frew me down? I'll mash you in de jaw if ye don't look out. I is no plantation nigger like you—I is a cullud gen'man.

POMP. You a cullud gen'man! Ough! you'se de ugliest nigger I ever saw.

JEFF (*recognizing him*). What! Eh! It is—No, it ain't—Yes, it is—

POMP. What! Jeff!

JEFF. Pompey! (*they embrace*) Why, you ugly moke, whar has you been?

POMP. I'se been in de wars.

JEFF. Glad to see you, broder in a sacred cause. (*aside*) I'll fool dis nigger.

POMP. Whar am you gwine wid dat portmantoo?

JEFF. Whar? I'se gwine to Kernel Woodruff's. You know whar it is, don't you? He's waiting fur it.

POMP. De Kernel's gwine to get spliced, ain't he?

JEFF. Not afore he gets dis ere portmantoo—his swaller-tail coat is in dar.

POMP. Come along—I'll help you tote it.

JEFF. No, you don't—dar's fifty cents in dis job.

POMP. Fifty cents? Golly, nigger, I'll tote it fur a quarter.

JEFF. Well, then, take it along, Buck.

POMP. (*taking up portmanteau*). Fifty cents! It's more money dan I'se seen in a month. Whar did you say? Kernel Woodruff's?

JEFF. Yes.

POMP. All right, nigger. [*Exit at* R.

JEFF. Ha! ha! ha! Dat nigger is a fool. He's gwine to carry that fur nuffin—ha! ha! ha!

Enter DAN *at* L., *in captain's uniform.*

DAN (*slapping* JEFF *on the shoulder*). Say, beautiful snow, which is the way to the church? or don't you know?

JEFF. Ough! (*recognizing him*) Beg pardon, Mr. Wildman. (*aside*) What brings him up dis way?

DAN. I'm waiting for an answer, and if you don't be particularly lively about it, I'll give you a dose of shoe leather.

JEFF. All right, boss. It's about a mile from here, right straight ahead on dat road. (*pointing* R.) I'se gwine dat way, and I'll show you de church.

DAN. Well, then, go ahead and I'll follow.

JEFF. All right, boss.   [*Exits*, R.

DAN. Now, to meet my darlings, and press them once more to my heart.   [*Exits*, R.

SCENE IV.—*Parlor in* MR. STEWART'S *home.*

Enter ALICE, *in wedding dress, and* MR. STEWART, R.

MR. STEWART. I have given you my consent long ago—and I will not take it back, now that you are about to give yourself to the man of your choice.

ALICE. Thank you, dear father—your words give me much cheer. Harry is good, noble and true.

MR S. As long as fortune smiles upon me, you may scorn to give even a thought to need—though Harry is poor——

ALICE. True, father, he is poor in what the world calls gold, but vastly rich in true love's devotion.

MR. S. And I would not bring any opposition to your choice—but reflect well—to-morrow might see me a poor man.—and then, you, my child, would, perhaps suffer privations, and it would break my heart.

ALICE. His ambition, his manly heart will not permit him to remain inactive, at least.

MR. S. Ambition seldom reaches the height of its aim, yet if Harry succeeds in civil, as he has in military life, he must attain fortune.

ALICE. Your words cheer me, dear father, as they did when I ventured amidst the dangers and annoyances of the war to attend to our sick and wounded boys.

MR. S. And I am doubly proud of you for the self-sacrificing part you took in the war. You're well worthy of the greatest hero.

ALICE. You will spoil me, dear father!

MR. S. (*kissing her*). There, there, you are a good child, and my wishes for your happiness go with you.

Enter FRIENDS, *etc.*

Our friends have come. The regiment will be waiting for us. Come.
                                                   [*All exit at back.*

SCENE V.—*A Street.*

Enter TIM, *on crutches,* CARL *and* JEFF, R.

TIM. Now, be aisy wid yer tongues, ye divils. Phat is it ye want wid Timothy O'Brien?

JEFF. We want you to see the wedding of Massa Kurnel Woodruff and Miss Stewart—dat's all, boss.

TIM. Be the powers of Bridget Mulcahey, is it de likes of ye dat Kurnel Woodruff would have at his wedding? Why, bad luck to ye, ye haven't got even a dacent pair of brogues on your feet.

JEFF. Brogues! Golly, do you take dis ere cullud pusson for an Irishman? (*goes to* L.)

TIM. Gorra! Go get de soot scraped out of yer face, ye son of a nager. The man dat'd take ye for an Irishman would take me for Quane Victoria! ain't dat so, Dutchy?

CARL. I don't know. I vas peen no pizziness mit dot fellah—Victorora.

TIM. Howld your whisht, man—I said Victoria. Ye're as big a dunce as dat black divil over there.

CARL. Oh! you vas peen a bad maus. Ven you got died, you vas peen gone py dot hot blaces——

TIM. Be the powers of war, I'd like to die the day you do.

CARL. How's dot?

TIM. Arrah! sure, the divil'd be so much taken up wid ye, he'd forget me intirely. But see, the regiment is coming this way.

[*All three exit*, L.

SCENE VI.—*Landscape at back. Church at* R. 3 E.

Enter RICHMOND, L. U. E., *stealthily.*

RICHMOND. This must be the church—I overheard some men say it is here they are to be married. So be it. It is a fine spot for an escape —and ere another hour rolls by, I will snatch the cup of bliss from their lips. I cannot have survived that terrible fall over the precipice to be foiled again. No—this time my vengeance will be swift, aye, swift as death. Then let the earth open, and, in its deep abyss, let it hide my despair. (*footsteps heard, and he disappears at* R., *behind the church.*)

Enter TIM, CARL *and* JEFF, L. 2 E.

CARL. Py cracious, Teem, you vas peen a pully poy. Of you vas peen a Yerman you vas peen a pully poyer.

TIM. Howld yer gab, Dutchy. I'd jist as soon be brother to dis nager, than be a Dutchman.

JEFF. You're right, boss.

TIM. And I'd jist as soon be a monkey at once than be such a bad imitation of one as ye are.

CARL. Pully, pully. Look owit Dot rechiments vas coming py dese places. Wourah!

Enter REGIMENT *at* L., *commanded by* COLONEL WOODRUFF, *who turns over the command to the* LIEUTENANT-COLONEL. *The* TROOPS *are massed in columns of Companies on left of stage, facing church, and brought to a rest.* HARRY *meets his father and mother, at* R. 2 E.; *they embrace.*

HARRY. Home at last, dear parents. (MR. *and* MRS. WOODRUFF, *after the embrace, seem to look for the absent son*) I understand you. Jack is not here. Alas—we must bow submissively to the will of the Almighty. His wife and children shall be ours to care for.

MR. W. There will be one vacant chair, and the dear one will be sadly missed; but we gave him to our country, and God took him to his care

MRS. W. Where, let us hope, we will some day meet him.

HAR. Till then, my good father and mother, I will try, by renewed devotion, to make you forget that we have lost him.

Mr. W. You have a noble heart, Harry; but see who comes!

Enter ALICE, *and her friends, including* DR. BOLUS, MR. STEWART, MRS. SANFORD, *and* MARY, R. 2 E.

HAR. Alice!

ALICE. Harry!

MR. S. Now, let us go into the church. (*organ begins to play, and all but* SOLDIERS *enter church, except* MRS. SANFORD *and* LITTLE MARY, *who stop in centre.*)

BEN. (*comes down to them*). Come, little girl, give me your hand. Be more cheerful, Mrs. Sanford. I'll jest take car●of ye—until Dan comes up this way, and then, by the 'tarnal, he can jest manœuvre his own command.

MRS. S. Thank you, sir; but will he soon come?

BEN. I can't zactly say, jest now, when he'll come; but, you bet he'll come, as long as he sed so. (MRS. SANFORD *and* MARY *enter church.*)

Enter MEHITABLE, *at* R. 2 E.

MEHITABLE. Why, Benny!

BEN. How are you, Mehit? (*kisses her*) Yours, truly. I'll be darned but you're jest in time. The minister is in there, and everything is ready—speak out; will you say the word?

MEHIT. Well, you're kind o' sudden in your way o' popping the question——

BEN. Pop be darned! I'm talking about business now; I've got no money—no good clothes—if you marry me you'll never be anything but a farmer's wife. Will you do it?

MEHIT. Well, I reckon I will. Come along.

BEN. (*to* SOLDIERS). Boys, I'm gone up.

SOLDIERS. Go it, Benny.

BEN. Yours, truly. (*enters church with* MEHITABLE.)

OFFICER (*commands*). Attention, Battalion! Shoulder arms! Present arms!

BRIDAL PARTY *enters from church; when* ALICE *and* HARRY *have reached the centre of the stage,* RICHMOND *enters,* R. 4 E., *from behind the church, with wild looks and dishevelled hair.*

RICHMOND Now, die, and take my curse. (*strikes at them with dagger. Movement of* HARRY *and* ALICE, *and screams of the latter.*)

Enter DAN, *with pistol,* R. 2 E., *fires at* RICHMOND, *who falls.*

DAN. Hold your hosses! I was watching you—guess that'll settle you!

OFFICER (*commands*). Shoulder arms! Right face! Forward march! Column left, march! (*taking position at back for tableau.*)

MRS. S. } Husband!

MARY. } Papa!

RICH. Curse you all! (*dies, and is carried off.*)

HAR. We owe you another debt of gratitude.

DAN. You owe me nothing since my darlings have found among you the home and comfort they could not find among their people. And we will bless you, and pray for your happiness in the life you have this day entered upon.

ALICE. Remain with us and your darlings will be ours.

DAN. Thanks; and now, may priceless peace, bought with a nation's blood, be forever permanent in the land!

Tableau : " Liberty."

END.

THE FLAG OF THE FREE.

BY H. MILLARD,

Author of " Viva l' America," etc.

PRINTED BY PERMISSION OF THE COMPOSER.

With Energy, and not too Fast.

No - bly our flag flutters o'er us to - day, Emblem of peace, pledge of lib - er - ty's sway; Its foes shall tremble and shrink in dis-may, If e'er in-sult-ed it be. Our *stripes and stars*, loved and honored by all, Shall float for ev - er where free - dom shall call; It still shall be the flag of the free, Emblem of sweet lib - er - ty.

CHORUS.

Here we will gather its cause to defend, Let patriots

ral - ly and wise counsels lend, It still shall be the

flag of the free, Em - blem of sweet lib - er - ty!

With it in beauty, no flag can compare,
All nations honor our banner so fair;
If to insult it, a traitor should *dare*,
    Crushed to the earth let him be!
" *Freedom and Progress* " our watchword to-day,
When duty calls us, who dares disobey?
Honor to thee, thou flag of the free,
    Emblem of sweet liberty!
       Chorus, etc.

Ever united, this fair land shall be,
Our flag shall conquer on land or on sea,
Every opposer shall soon bend the knee,
    Good speed the darling old flag!
No North, no South, no New England, no West,
One country always, the greatest, the best;
Long may it wave—the poor and opprest
    Bless thee, thou flag of the free!
       Chorus, etc.

STAGE DIRECTIONS.

R. means Right of Stage, facing the Audience; L. Left; C. Centre; R. C. Right of Centre; L. C. Left of Centre. D. F. Door in the Flat, or Scene running across the back of the Stage; C. D. F. Centre Door in the Flat; R. D. F. Right Door in the Flat; L. C. F. Left Door in the Flat; R. D. Right Door; L. D. Left Door; 1 E. First Entrance; 2 E. Second Entrance; U. E. Upper Entrance; 1, 2 or 3 G. First Second or Third Groove.

R.   R. C.   C.   R. C.   L.

☞ The reader is supposed to be upon the stage facing the audience.